SHOTS
FIRED

Center Point
Large Print

Also by C. J. Box and available from Center Point Large Print:

Breaking Point

This Large Print Book carries the Seal of Approval of N.A.V.H.

C. J. BOX

SHOTS FIRED

Stories from JOE PICKETT Country

CENTER POINT LARGE PRINT
THORNDIKE, MAINE

This Center Point Large Print edition is published
in the year 2014 by arrangement with Blue Rider Press,
a member of Penguin Group (USA) LLC,
a Penguin Random House Company.

Additional copyright information on page 303.

The text of this Large Print edition is unabridged.
In other aspects, this book may vary from the original edition.
Printed in the United States of America on permanent paper.
Set in 16-point Times New Roman type.

ISBN: 978-1-62899-236-6

Library of Congress Cataloging-in-Publication Data

Box, C. J.
[Short stories. Selections]
Shots fired : stories from Joe Pickett Country / C. J. Box. —
    Center Point Large Print edition.
pages ; cm
Summary: "Suspense stories about the Wyoming that Box knows so
well—and the dark deeds and impulses that can be found there"
—Provided by publisher.
ISBN 978-1-62899-236-6 (library binding : alk. paper)
1. Pickett, Joe (Fictitious character)—Fiction.
    2. Game wardens—Fiction. 3. Wyoming—Fiction.
    4. Large type books. I. Title.
PS3552.O87658A6 2014b
813'.54—dc23
                                                        2014025776

CONTENTS

INTRODUCTION

The short stories in this collection were written over the last decade and appeared here and there—as limited editions, in obscure anthologies, or not at all. Three of them ("One-Car Bridge," "Blood Knot," "Shots Fired") are new and original to this anthology.

I've received many inquiries over the years from readers asking where they could find the stories, and thanks to the good folks at Penguin/Putnam (especially my legendary editor, Neil Nyren), *here they are*. All of them. Four feature Joe Pickett and/or Nate Romanowski ("One-Car Bridge," "The Master Falconer," "Dull Knife," "Shots Fired") and the rest are wide-ranging, from the Wind River Mountains, Wyoming Territory, 1835 ("The End of Jim and Ezra") to a dark little number in modern-day Paris via South Dakota ("Le Sauvage Noble"). Also included are pieces set in Yellowstone ("Pirates of Yellowstone"), the North Platte River in Wyoming ("Every Day Is a Good Day on the River"—one of my firmest beliefs, by the way), and during a ferocious Wyoming blizzard ("Pronghorns of the Third Reich").

There's a question that always comes up at talks and book signings, which is: "Where do you get your ideas?" It's the most confounding question for a writer to answer, I think, and leads to an answer that is unsatisfactory for the person who queried. It's as if when one revealed the *true* (but obviously withheld) answer, the curtain would be pulled back and the secret would be out.

I've always thought that the components of writing a novel are ninety-five percent craft and five percent creativity. I can respond to questions about craft just like a carpenter can talk about specific tools and tricks of the trade. Writing a book is like anything: One goes to work in the morning, every morning, and writes. Pages come out. Eventually, there are enough pages to make it a novel.

What I can't answer well is where the five percent comes from, or how to pull it from the air. It's just *there*—or it isn't.

What follows are brief introductions to each story: where they appeared, why they were written, and where the ideas came from.

"One-Car Bridge" is a new Joe Pickett story that appears here for the first time. It derived from a dinner conversation over drinks with a third-generation rancher whose grandfather was notoriously tough on his employees—so tough that his legacy still hovers over the land like a black cloud.

"Pirates of Yellowstone" first appeared in an anthology called *Meeting Across the River*, where the editors asked a number of writers to contribute short stories based on the Bruce Springsteen song of the same name. I puzzled over what I would write, since I don't do gritty urban. Hank Williams, sure. Bob Wills, maybe. But the Boss? I was thinking this over one evening in Gardiner, Montana, within sight of Yellowstone Park, when I witnessed several black-leather-clad Eastern European types in street shoes smoking cigarettes outside a local bar. They fit into the rough outdoorsy atmosphere like gangbangers at a cattle branding. I found out they'd been recruited overseas to work inside the park but there weren't enough jobs available when they arrived. So I speculated on what kind of job—and trouble—they might get into.

Nobody—oh, maybe ten people—read "The End of Jim and Ezra" when it appeared in an anthology called *Geezer Noir II* a few years ago. In fact, I've never even seen a copy of the book. The volume was withdrawn from the market due to legal issues that resulted from the tragic early death of its publisher, David Thompson—one of the truly good and brilliant men in the world of booksellers. David was the marketing director and friend to all at Murder By The Book in Houston, one of my favorite stores. The story took David by surprise because he was expecting something contemporary, not a piece about two mountain-men friends set in 1835. But he liked it very much and he urged me—someday—to write a historical novel set in the same period. We'll see. Anybody who has spent too much time with a business partner will relate to Jim and Ezra.

"The Master Falconer" appeared as a limited-edition short story published by ASAP in California and was available to fewer than a few hundred collectors. Later, it was released as an e-story. The piece is the first time I tackled a tale centered entirely on Nate Romanowski, the outlaw falconer from the Joe Pickett series. I wanted to see if I could do it and also see if Nate could carry a story on his own. I liked the results, and it set the stage for *Force of Nature* later in the series. Plus, I was angry at the Saudi royal family.

"Every Day Is a Good Day on the River" was my contribution to an anthology of fishing stories written by crime writers called *Hook, Line & Sinister*. It was edited by my friend and fishing buddy T. Jefferson Parker and contained entries from Michael Connelly, Ridley Pearson, Don Winslow, James W. Hall, and others. There is some great stuff in it. The proceeds of the book went to Casting for Recovery, helping women cancer survivors, and Project Healing Waters, which assists returning veterans. Two great causes. The setting is a cold day on the North Platte River north of Casper, Wyoming. There are three men in the drift boat—two clients, a guide—and a gun.

"Pronghorns of the Third Reich" (my second-favorite title next to "Every Day Is a Good Day . . .") is an example of how short stories are birthed at times in disconnected, disparate, and mysterious ways. In this case, there are two main ingredients that went into the pot to create a dark little stew. First, Otto Penzler, owner of the Mysterious Bookshop in New York and unofficial czar of the mystery book universe, asked me to contribute a piece for a series of small books he was publishing using bibliophiles—book collectors—as the theme. Second, I was doing some research at the American Heritage Center at the University of Wyoming when I stumbled on a single photo in the Charles Belden collection taken in 1936 that simply took my breath away. (Belden was a fascinating rancher and photographer based near Meeteetse, Wyoming.) I still stare at the photo and shake my head. But whatever you do, don't spoil the surprise for yourself. Read the story and don't jump ahead to that last page.

"Dull Knife" was the first Joe Pickett short story for ASAP (see above) and came from an incident I recalled years before while ice-fishing with my father on Ocean Lake in Central Wyoming. There were four or five of us boys, and our job was to check the holes every hour throughout the night to see if there was a fish on the baited hook. One night, in the distance across the frozen surface of the lake, we saw a mysterious glow from under the ice. We had no explanation for the phenomenon and our speculation ranged from underwater vessels (ridiculous) to UFOs (even more so) to something supernatural. Later, we discovered that the glow was the result of dying headlights of a completely submerged car that had crashed through the surface at night and sunk to the bottom. There were no fatalities, and we never learned how the car got there. Joe Pickett, of course, doggedly investigates this eerie accident in this story.

"Le Sauvage Noble" ("The Noble Savage") is easily one of the most exuberantly twisted and cynical stories I've ever written. Again, this was for ASAP. The germ of an idea that later fueled the story occurred at, of all places, the American embassy in the heart of Paris. I was there as part of a contingent of state tourism representatives in France to host a dinner and cocktail party for travel agents and journalists who, we hoped, would write about the Rocky Mountain West or send clients there. I found myself standing next to two American Indians in full native dress. Since they weren't from any of our states, I asked why they were there. It was because, they said with a wink, French women liked the idea of having sex with Native Americans, and they never missed an embassy reception. The reason made me whoop. The next night we attended the Wild West Show at Disneyland Paris, which somehow confirmed what the Indians had said and revealed something about the French I never would have imagined. You might need to take a shower after this one.

"Blood Knot" is the shortest of short stories: one thousand words. Why? Because a newspaper in the United Kingdom requested it, accepted it, and sent a check. But for whatever reason they never ran it, and no one has read it until now. Because of the limitation on the word count, it was a challenge honing this multigenerational encounter down to size. I couldn't waste a word. And I like the results.

"Shots Fired: A Requiem for Ander Esti" is a Joe Pickett short story written solely for this anthology. It's about dirtbags encountered in the middle of nowhere that bring about a sense of loss to Joe that almost overwhelms him. The impetus for the tale comes from an experience of my own many years before when I worked summers on an exploration survey crew based out of Casper, Wyoming. Our job (I was the lowly rodman) was to re-survey corners and bench-marks in the practically roadless Powder River Basin near Pumpkin Buttes. It turned out the location for the stake we needed to drive into the ground happened to be *exactly* beneath the only man-made structure within sight: a sheep wagon.

The odds against something like that happening were incredible. Nevertheless, it was my job to approach this lonely wagon of a sheepherder who had likely not seen another human in weeks and knock on the door . . .

I hope you enjoy reading these stories as much as I enjoyed writing them.

C. J. Box
Wyoming, 2014

ONE-CAR BRIDGE

The tires of Joe Pickett's green Ford Wyoming Game and Fish Department pickup thumped rhythmically across the one-car bridge that spanned the Twelve Sleep River. Ahead was the Crazy Z Bar Ranch. Joe was there to deliver bad news to the ranch manager.

It was Saturday in early September during the two-week period between the end of summer in the high country and preceding hunting season openers. The morning had started off with the bite of fall but had warmed by the hour. The groves of aspens in the mountains were already turning gold, although the cottonwoods flanking both sides of the river still held green and full. The river was down but still floatable, and upriver in the distance he caught a glimpse of a low-profile McKenzie-style drift boat rounding a bend. The guide manned the oars, and fly-fishermen clients cast from the front and back of the boat, long sweeps of fly-line catching the sun, toward a deep seam near the far bank.

He held his breath as he did every time he drove across. There were gaps between the two-by-eights that made up the surface of the bridge and he could see glimpses of the river flash by through his open driver's-side window. The bridge itself was over forty-five years old and constructed of steel girders held together by bolts. Auburn tears of rust flowed down the surface of the steel and pooled in the channels of the I-beams, which had long ago inspired a local fishing guide to deem it "the Bridge of Cries." It stuck.

Out of view beneath the bridge hung a large metal hand-painted sign:

THIS IS PRIVATE PROPERTY
FISHERMEN, STAY IN YOUR BOAT
VIOLATORS WILL BE PROSECUTED
BY THE CRAZY Z BAR RANCH

Joe knew from experience they weren't kidding. Even that time in high water when a raft filled with Boy Scouts capsized on the swells and rocks. Eight sodden but uninjured Scouts and their two Scoutmasters—one with a broken arm— had found the ranch headquarters at dusk. The former manager, following standing orders from the owner, loaded them all into the bed of his three-quarter-ton pickup and drove them to the Saddlestring jail to press charges.

The absentee owner of the ranch, Lamar Dietrich of St. Louis, had the signs put up when he bought the ranch. He meant what he said and played for keeps. And he wouldn't be happy at all, Joe knew, to hear why Joe had come.

• • •

Daisy, Joe's two-year-old Labrador, raised her head from where she slept on the passenger seat to stare at the Angus cattle that grazed on the side of the dirt road. She was fascinated with cows, and Joe wondered if in Daisy's mind cows appeared to her as very large black dogs. A tremulous whine came from deep in her throat.

"Settle down," Joe said, navigating a turn and plunging his truck through a thin spring creek that crossed the road. "Don't even think about chasing them."

Daisy looked over at him with a puzzled expression.

"Chasing Dietrich's cattle is a death sentence. He's had dogs shot for it. I want to keep you around for a while."

Daisy lowered her head.

"He's got a big binder he calls *The Book of Rules* that sits on a table in the foreman's house," Joe said to Daisy. "I've seen it, and it's thick. He expects every one of his ranch managers to memorize it, and he has tabs for every conceivable circumstance and how they're supposed to deal with it. He's got tabs on trespassing and road improvement and cattle management and fifty or so other tabs on everything he can think of. If the ranch manager makes a decision that isn't covered in *The Book of Rules*, that manager doesn't stay around very long. There's a tab on stray dogs. They're to be shot on sight so they don't run his cattle.

"So keep your head down, especially if Dietrich is around," Joe said. "He's just plain mean."

Joe had met Dietrich two times over the years, and both encounters were unpleasant. The old man was in his late seventies and appeared shorter than he actually was because his back was stooped and his shoulders slumped forward. Because of the deformity, his head was always down and when he looked up his eyes appeared menacing. His voice was a low soft growl and he didn't waste words. He had no time or respect for local officials, state game wardens, or incompetent ranch foremen.

Joe had heard that Dietrich had amassed his fortune by negotiating cutthroat deals with urban governments for waste management services. There were thousands of distinctive red-and-yellow Dietrich Waste Management trucks throughout the inner cities of the Rust Belt and the northeastern states. He'd taken on local political machines and organized crime families to secure long-term contracts. Then, like so many extremely wealthy men in America, he had looked around for a safe haven for his cash and opted to sink some of it in real estate and had chosen to buy massive ranches in the West, including this one in Wyoming. The Crazy Z Bar, with tens of thousands of acres of mountainous terrain, pastureland, sagebrush flats, and fifteen premium miles of the Twelve Sleep River snaking through it. The purchase price, Joe had heard, was $22.5 million.

The first time Joe met Dietrich was when the then-foreman of the ranch, under orders from the owner, had strung barbed wire across the river to stop the passage of local fishing guides and recreational floaters. Joe had explained that state law allowed access to all navigable waters, that the land itself was private—even the river bottom itself—but the water was public. As long as the boaters didn't anchor or step out of their boat, they could legally cross the ranch. Dietrich exploded and ordered his then-foreman to beat up Joe right there and then. The foreman refused, and was fired. Joe filed charges against Dietrich for threatening him, but dropped them when Dietrich agreed to remove his barbed-wire fence.

The second time, just two months ago, Joe was at a hearing before the Game and Fish Commission on a plan Dietrich proposed to convert two thousand acres of his ranch into a wild game hunting operation. Dietrich's idea was to import water buffalo, gazelles, kudu, blackbuck, and scimitar-horned oryx from Africa to be hunted by his friends. Since Joe was the local game warden, he was asked to testify, and he testified against the plan. Exotic, non-native species were a threat to the antelope, deer, and elk populations, he had said, and there was no way for Dietrich to guarantee the animals would never escape or pass along diseases that could decimate local wildlife. Dietrich appeared briefly at the hearing and extended a crooked finger at Joe and called him "a no-account tinhorn jackbooted thug."

Joe said: "I've never been called that before."

Because the atmosphere in the hearing room was so poisonous, the commission chose to take the decision under advisement and issue a ruling at a future date.

That date had arrived. They had voted no. And Joe was tasked with delivering the verdict to the new ranch manager of the Crazy Z Bar, the Dietrich employee who had drafted and presented the proposal, Kyle Sandford.

Poor Kyle, Joe thought.

Although Lamar Dietrich's magnificent empty home—built of native stone and sheets of glass so heavy and large that they'd been delivered by a cargo helicopter—was set into the side of the mountain that overlooked the river bottom, the manager's house was humble and in need of paint and new shingles. It was located on a sagebrush shelf with a cluster of outbuildings including a metal barn, corrals, and a Quonset hut for housing vehicles and machinery.

There was never any need to knock on the doors of ranch homes, and no way to sneak onto a ranch. Daisy perked up again when a gaggle of motley ranch dogs boiled out from pools of shade and streaked toward Joe's pickup. They formed yipping, tumbling knots on both sides and accompanied him as he drove into the ranch yard, nipping at the tires and fenders, the cacophony signaling the arrival of a stranger.

"You stay," Joe said to Daisy over the racket.

The three members of the Sandford family appeared from three different places in the ranch yard as if joining each other on a stage: Joleen came from the ranch house itself, drying her hands on a dish towel; Kyle Sr. looked out from the Quonset, gripping a Crescent wrench with an oily hand; and Kyle Jr. strolled from a pocket of willows that marked the bank of the river, his fly rod poking nine feet into the air.

Joe was most familiar with Kyle Jr., who was seventeen and ran in the same circle as his ward, April. He was a quiet ranch kid who had boarded the same bus as other ranch kids until he could drive himself, but hadn't been in the valley long enough—and wasn't an outstanding athlete, scholar, or leader—to belong firmly to a pack. He seemed like a floater, the kind of boy who hung back and to the side, keeping his mouth shut, occasionally surprising others with a good quip or an observation, but was never missed when he didn't show up and never mentioned when groups were forming to attend games, go out on Friday nights, or plan a party. Joe recalled April reviewing digital photos of her friends at a football game, pointing out characters and laughing about things they'd done or said. When she came across a photo of Kyle Sandford Jr., she shook her head and said, "I don't remember him being there, but I guess he was."

Kyle Jr. was wiry and dark with a prominent Adam's apple and wispy sideburns. Joe had never seen the boy smile, but he had eyes that seemed to carefully take everything in.

Kyle Sr. nodded a reserved hello to Joe and Joe nodded back. Joleen withdrew into the house but stood behind the screen, watching carefully. Kyle Sr. tossed his wrench into a bucket of tools behind him, clamped on a dirty short-brimmed Stetson Rancher, and greeted Joe by saying, "Joe."

"Hello, Kyle."

"Did you bring me some good news?"

Joe paused. "Nope."

Kyle Sr. took a deep breath and stood still. His face betrayed nothing, but Joe saw Joleen shake her head behind the screen and turn away.

"It was unanimous," Joe said. "The commission voted to not allow a game farm. They said it would be a bad precedent, even if your owner did all the security fencing and inoculations he said he would."

Kyle Sr. said nothing. He just stared at Joe and his mouth got tight.

Finally, in a thin voice, he said, "Is there any-thing we can do about this?"

Joe was puzzled. Was Kyle Sr. offering a bribe? "Like what?"

"Make another run at 'em, maybe. Adjust the proposal so they're happy about it this time, you know?"

Joe shook his head. "They'll meet again in a month, but I can't see them changing their minds."

Kyle Sr. dropped his head and stared at the top of his boots. "You know what's going to happen then, right?" he asked.

"I'm guessing Lamar Dietrich won't be too happy," Joe said.

Kyle Sr. snorted and said, "You got that right. But you know what else will happen?"

Joe said he didn't.

"Come with me," Kyle Sr. said, gesturing with his chin toward the house. "I'll show you some-thing."

Joe started forward and remembered Kyle Jr. He looked over at the boy as he passed by. "Any luck?" he asked.

"They're hitting on prince nymphs and scuds."

"Any size to 'em?"

"Eighteen, nineteen inches," Kyle Jr. said. "I broke off one that was bigger than that."

"Nice fish," Joe said, impressed.

"Yeah," Kyle Jr. said, his eyes worried, "they were."

Inside, Kyle Sr. pointed toward *The Book of Rules* and Joe knew then what was coming. The man slid the binder across the counter and used a greasy thumb to find the right tab. Joe read it: LOCAL POLITICAL INFLUENCE.

Kyle Sr. folded back the tab to the first page of the section, and read:

" 'As Ranch Manager of the Crazy Z Bar, an important part of your responsibilities is to develop influential working relationships with officials on the county and state level. The purpose of these relationships is to further the goals of the property and implement projects deemed important by the owner. Failure to secure beneficial results and decisions may result in termination.' "

Joe contemplated that.

Kyle Sr. said, "Mr. Dietrich thinks anything is possible if you've got the right relationships with the powers that be. That's how he got to be such a rich man. He thinks all his managers need to have that same ability. I guess I don't."

"It's not that," Joe said. "I was at the hearing, remember?"

"And you testified against us."

"Yes, I did. But it wasn't because the proposal was sloppy or you weren't a good man making a strong bid. The game farm was rejected on its merits. It would have been the only game farm in the whole state, and policy was against you from the start. I think we have a lot of stupid policies, but that isn't one of them. No one wants to be out elk hunting and run into a water buffalo. Simple as that."

"I know," Kyle Sr. said softly. "But that won't matter to Mr. Dietrich. He'll see it as me being a piss-poor influencer of mucky-mucks. He won't look at the big picture and see how I've made our cattle operation go into the black or how I've sold more hay than any other manager here over the years. He'll look at this tab and cut me loose."

Joe said, "He can't be that unreasonable."

"You don't know him like I do," Kyle Sr. said, shaking his head. "If someone doesn't do the job he wants, he cuts 'em loose. Haven't you ever wondered why this place has gone through six managers in fifteen years? I've stuck the longest —going on four years. But he'll find out about this decision and—"

Joe looked up when Kyle Sr. suddenly stopped talking to see what had stopped him. He followed the man's eyes to the outside screen door, where Kyle Jr. stood on the porch.

Joe understood. No father wanted his son to think of him as a failure, whether the circumstances were fair or not.

"We're talking," Kyle Sr. said to Kyle Jr.

"Are we gonna have to move again?" the boy asked.

Kyle Sr. raised his voice and said, "I said we're talking in here, son. I don't need you standing there listening in. You go get the company truck and gas it up. You can take it into town."

Kyle Jr. looked back, uncomprehending. "Why?" he asked.

"Because Mr. Dietrich is coming for his quarterly visit. You can pick him up and bring him out here."

"Why me?" Kyle Jr. asked, pain in his eyes.

"Because your mother and me need to start packing up," Kyle Sr. said.

From the living room, out of sight, Joe heard Joleen gasp.

To her, Kyle Sr. said, "You'll be getting what you always wanted, Joleen."

She responded with a choked mewl.

To Joe, he said as an aside, "She never liked this place, anyhow. She's scared of Dietrich and she'd like to be closer to her people in Idaho. Maybe we'll end up there now."

"What about Kyle Junior?" Joe asked, after the boy had left the porch.

"He loves this place," he said with a heavy sigh. "He thought we'd finally found a place for him where we could stay awhile. He's made some friends and he's finally getting settled in. Now we're going to jerk him out of high school and hit the road again."

Joe shook his head.

"He ain't never stayed in a place for more than a year or two," Kyle Sr. said. "He's like an army brat, I guess. But for some reason he thought this one would take. He finally let his guard down and started making connections. He told us he really likes it—the town, the school, even his teachers. Now . . ." He didn't finish the sentence.

As Joe opened the door to go back out to his pickup, Kyle Sr. said, "Old man Dietrich couldn't have better timing. He's showing up on the day we find out about the game farm decision. He won't even have a chance to cool off before he fires me. He likes doing it face-to-face. He says that's the only way to fire a man: face-to-face. It's in *The Book of Rules.*"

"How's he getting here?" Joe asked.

"Kyle Junior is picking him up."

"No, I meant to Saddlestring?"

"Private plane," Kyle Sr. said. "He must have brought the jet or he'd land on our own strip."

"How many planes does he have?"

"Three that I know of."

Joe said, "Maybe I'll meet him at the airport along with Kyle Junior. I'll tell him the news and make sure he knows it had nothing to do with you. Maybe that will help."

Kyle Sr. smiled bitterly. "Worth a try, I guess." But Joe could tell he wasn't optimistic.

As Joe descended the stairs on the porch, he heard Kyle Sr. say to Joleen: "I'll hitch up the horse trailer and back it up to the front door. You start gathering our personal stuff. Mr. Dietrich has been known to give folks an hour to clean out. We might need more than that . . ."

Joe swung into the truck and said to Daisy, "Man oh man."

Daisy lowered her head between her big paws on the seat. Joe reached for his keys as Kyle Jr. drove through the ranch yard in the Crazy Z Bar's Ford F-350. Joe got a glimpse of the boy's face. He looked stricken.

As Joe crossed the one-car bridge and drove toward Saddlestring in the lingering dust spoor of the F-350, he thought of the ranches in the Twelve Sleep River valley. There were twenty or more big holdings, most owned by out-of-state executives. But beyond that fact, each was mightily different from the other.

In his experience, each ranch was a world of its own: teeming with intrigue, agendas, and characters. Each was a fiefdom with its own peculiarities and practices, its own set of rules and expectations. Ranch managers were itinerants in cowboy hats who did the bidding of their owners but, unlike the owners, had to interact with the locals. They hired cooks, wranglers, cowboys, and hands who specialized in construction, fixing fences, and wildlife management. Their employees gossiped about them, and sometimes switched ranches for better deals or benefits. There was lots of interbreeding, and relationships formed between employees of one ranch and employees of others. Even for Joe, who was out among them day after day, it was hard to keep it all straight.

Despite telephones, email, and the Internet, most of the information and rumors from ranch to ranch were communicated daily through snippets of information relayed to the ranch communities by those who kept an old-fashioned circuit of visits, like brand inspectors, cattle buyers, large-animal veterinarians, and the almost legendary mail lady named Sandra "Asperger" Hamburger, who had delivered the mail in the rural areas on an ironclad timetable that had not wavered more than five minutes each day for fifteen years. Hamburger was unmarried and in her mid-sixties, and favored brightly colored cowboy shirts, jeans, short gray hair, and steel-framed cat-eye glasses she'd worn for so many years they were in fashion again. She was a tightly wrapped eccentric with mild autism—hence her nickname —who drove an ancient mud-spattered Dodge Power Wagon. She could be counted on to arrive at each rural mailbox on schedule, every day, despite the conditions. To her, the U.S. Postal Service was an all-powerful god and she didn't want to let it down. When she was running late by even a few minutes, she was a terror. When Joe saw Hamburger's truck barreling down a two-track road, raising dust behind her, he simply pulled over and let her pass. Otherwise, he was taking his life in his hands.

But if Joe needed information or intel on any of the ranch managers or their employees, Sandra Asperger Hamburger was who he sought out. She knew all the names, most of their backgrounds, and most of their likes and dislikes based on what they sent or received in the mail. Often and intuitively, she knew of management shake-ups before anyone else in the valley. She wasn't a gossip, but she made it her business to know what was going on. Otherwise, she apparently reasoned, it might make her less efficient.

Some ranch managers fit right in, some contributed to the general welfare, and some were out-and-out bastards who used their positions as perches of power. A few of the ranch managers in the area were incompetent in every aspect of ranching other than being obsequious to the owner and his family when they arrived annually or semiannually, and that seemed to be enough to keep their jobs. Others were hardheaded cowmen who challenged their owners over budgets and priorities as if their roles were reversed. They didn't last long.

Kyle Sandford Sr., it seemed to Joe, was one of the good ones. He kept to himself—too much, apparently, for his own good—and honored local traditions and idiosyncrasies, or at least as much as *The Book of Rules* would let him. He was a member of the local Lions Club and he attended school activities with Joleen. Sandford managed the ranch as if it were his own, and he drove hard but fair bargains with cattle buyers, shippers, and local businesses. He didn't make dubious wildlife damage claims like some of the managers did, and he looked the other way when old-timers hunted or fished on private land they'd used for years.

Poor Kyle Sr., Joe thought. *And poor Kyle Jr.*

The Saddlestring Municipal Airport was located on a high plateau south of town. There were two commercial flights daily—both to Denver—and most of the activity at the airfield was as a fixed-base operator for private aircraft. The ranch Ford was parked in front of the small FBO building, and Joe swung into the lot and parked beside it. As he did, he heard the whine of a small plane accelerate in volume in the sky as it descended.

Joe swung out and patted Daisy on the head and pulled on his hat. Between two massive cumulus clouds to the east there was a glint of reflected light and it didn't take long for the speck to grow wings and wheels.

Inside the airport, Kyle Jr. sat on a molded plastic chair and stared out the windows at the tarmac. He wore a gray Saddlestring High School hoodie, worn jeans, cowboy boots, and a Wyoming Cowboys baseball cap. It was the official uniform of every teenage boy in town, Joe thought, except for the Goths and the druggies. Kyle Jr.'s hands rested on the tops of his thighs and his head was tilted slightly to the side, as if holding it erect took too much energy.

"Are you okay?" Joe asked.

Kyle Jr. started to respond, then apparently thought better of it.

"I know this must be tough. You kind of like it here, don't you?"

Kyle Jr. nodded his head.

"It's a good place," Joe said. "I know my girls would hate to leave it now that they're in high school. But maybe it won't come to that."

The boy looked up with hope in his eyes. "My dad didn't seem to think so."

Joe nodded. "I'm going to talk to Mr. Dietrich. Your dad is a hell of a hand. He would have a hard time replacing him. I can't believe he'd let him go because of something that was completely out of his control. I'll let him blame me."

"Thanks, I guess," Kyle Jr. said, letting his eyes linger on Joe for a second before looking away.

The sleek Piaggio Avanti II twin-engine turbo-prop sliced out of the wide blue sky and touched down on the single runway with the grace of a raptor snagging a fish. It turned and roared and wheeled straight toward the FBO, then performed a quick half-turn so the door faced the building.

Joe could see the outlines of two pilots wearing peaked caps in the cockpit, and once the aircraft was stopped one of the heads disappeared and ducked toward the back.

A sliding door whooshed to the side and steel stairs telescoped to the surface. The copilot filled the open hatch for a moment, looking out as if to assess any threats, then retreated back inside.

"Here he comes," Kyle Jr. said solemnly.

Lamar Dietrich, wearing a battered wide-brimmed hat and an oversized jacket, made his way slowly down the stairs. At the bottom he paused and reached back without turning his head, and the copilot scrambled down behind him and handed him a metal cane with three stubby feet on the bottom. Dietrich nodded toward the FBO but didn't move. The pilot danced around the old man and jogged toward a golf cart, then drove it out so Dietrich wouldn't have to walk.

The old man seemed even smaller than Joe remembered him, as if he'd folded over even more on himself. His shoulders seemed narrower although the large jacket disguised how frail he'd become. He wore lizard-skin boots that poked out from baggy khakis and he braced the walker over his thighs as the copilot delivered him to the building. Joe caught a glimpse of an overlarge gargoyle-like head, swinging jowls, and a large, sharp nose when Dietrich glanced up to see where they were going.

The electric cart made no sound as it approached the metal door of the FBO, but it obviously took a long moment for Dietrich to climb out. The copilot stepped inside sharply and held the door open for him.

Joe stood and jammed his hands in the front pockets of his jeans and braced himself.

Dietrich entered slowly and bent forward, using the walker with each step. He had bowed legs, which made him even shorter, Joe thought. He wondered how tall Dietrich was if he could be stretched out.

The old man paused and looked up, literally tilting his head until the back brim of his hat brushed his hunched shoulders. His eyes were hooded, and they took in Kyle Jr. still sitting in his chair and then Joe. When he recognized the game warden as the man who had testified at the hearing, his face hardened.

"You," Dietrich said. "I remember you. What the hell are you doing here?"

"Came to say howdy and welcome back," Joe said. "I was hoping I could have a minute of your time before you head out to your place."

"I don't have time for you," Dietrich said. He spoke in a hard and flat Midwestern tone that seemed like steel balls being dropped on concrete, Joe thought. Then, looking around the room, Dietrich said, "Where's Sandford?"

"I'm Kyle Junior," the boy said, leaping up.

"My dad asked me to give you a ride to the ranch."

Dietrich's eyes got larger as he assessed Kyle Jr. He obviously didn't like what he saw.

"How old are you?"

"Seventeen."

"Sandford sent a seventeen-year-old *boy* to pick me up?"

"I'm a good driver," Kyle Jr. said. "I've been driving since I was fourteen."

"This is unacceptable," Dietrich said. "I said I wanted Sandford here. Not his boy."

Kyle Jr. obviously didn't know what to say, and his face flushed red.

Joe stepped in and touched Dietrich on the shoulder. "Please, I'd like a minute if I could." Then to Kyle Jr.: "Why don't you step outside, Kyle?"

The boy was out the front door immediately, and Dietrich looked angrily to Joe for an explanation.

"Look," Joe said, "I know about you. You can't be as mean as you come off. You run a tight ship and you're a success in business, and I admire that. I disagree with your idea of building a game farm, but I admire your success and you've got a good ranch manager in Kyle Sandford. The decision on the game farm went against you. It wouldn't have mattered—"

Dietrich interrupted to say, "What a man does with his private property is his business. This isn't Communist China—yet. No bunch of bureaucrats have the right to tell me I can't do with my own property what I want to do."

"Actually, they do," Joe said. "And it isn't about what you do on your property, it's what happens if those exotic species get *off* your property. But that's only partially why I'm here—to tell you their decision face-to-face. I also need to let you know that the decision of the commission had nothing to do with Kyle. They liked him, and they thought the proposal he presented was as well done as any man could do. It was all based on the merits, not on the proposal."

Dietrich stared into Joe's eyes so long, Joe thought he'd have to blink first. And he did.

Dietrich said, "Merits. *Merits.* Do you realize how many times I've heard bullshit reasons like *merits* in my life? Nothing has to do with merits. Every decision has to do with respect and a little bit of fear."

Dietrich held up a thin bony hand and slowly clenched it. "Merits melt away when there's a fist behind the proposal. *Anything* is possible if you know how to play the game. That's the way of the world. Always has been, always will be. I need men who know how to play the game. I'd trade a thousand Kyle Sandfords for *one* Lamar Dietrich."

Joe said, "Maybe there is only one Lamar Dietrich. Did you ever think of that?"

Dietrich beheld Joe and for a moment Joe

thought the old man might smile. Instead, he quickly shook his head, as if purging an unpleasant thought.

"I need men I can trust and who can get the job done. I surround myself with winners. That's my secret. I don't have time or sympathy for losers.

"And I don't have time for you," Dietrich said, dismissing Joe with a wave of his hand.

"Just give him some time to make it right," Joe said to Dietrich's shuffling back. "He's putting roots down here and his son is in high school. It's not Kyle's fault you want something impossible to happen. Give him a reasonable project and he'll get it done. He's a good man."

"Losers stay losers," Dietrich said over his shoulder. "They don't ever make it right. Now where's that stupid boy?"

Joe stood in silence. He was played out. He watched Dietrich exit the building, wave his walker at Kyle Jr., and climb in the ranch pickup.

He heard about the accident over the mutual aid channel of his truck's radio. A pickup had plunged into the Twelve Sleep River off the one-car bridge at the Crazy Z Bar Ranch. There was one, and possibly two, fatalities. Joe tossed the sandwich he was eating out the driver's-side window and put his pickup into gear. He roared up the hill and past the airport and hit his emergency flashers when he cleared town.

• • •

The scene at the bridge told him most of what he wanted to know: The Ford F-350 was on its side in the river and the current flowed around and through it, cables on the right side of the bridge had been snapped by the impact and dangled from the I-beams, a sheriff's department SUV was parked haphazardly on Joe's side of the bridge, Kyle Sr.'s personal pickup was parked on the other, and in the middle of the bridge itself was Sandra Hamburger's Dodge Power Wagon.

"Jesus, help us," Joe whispered to Daisy.

Deputy Justin Woods climbed out of his SUV as Joe pulled up behind it. His uniform was wet from the shoulders down and his eyes looked haunted.

"You gotta help me, Joe," he said. "I was able to pull the boy out of the truck but I can't find the passenger down there."

"Is the boy okay?" Joe asked, swinging out of the pickup, followed by Daisy.

"He says he is," Woods said, nodding toward a bundled figure in the backseat. "He says Lamar Dietrich was in the truck with him. Fuckin' *Lamar Dietrich.*"

As they descended through the brush toward the river, Joe looked across. Joleen and Kyle Sr. stood near their pickup. Joleen was consoling a wailing Sandra Hamburger, trying to hug her to calm her down. Kyle Sr. stood with his hands on his hips and a terrified look on his face.

"Kyle Junior's okay!" Joe shouted.

"Thank God," Kyle Sr. replied, his shoulders suddenly relaxing with relief.

"So what did he say happened here?" Joe asked Woods.

"He said he picked up old man Dietrich at the airport and he was bringing him out here. He said he was crossing the bridge when he looked up and saw Sandra Hamburger coming straight at him, going fast. It was either hit her head-on or take it off the bridge, and he took it off the bridge."

Joe winced. Sandra's wails cut through the rushing sounds of the river.

"I cut him out of his seat belt," Woods said, "but I guess the old man wasn't wearing his."

Joe nodded and they plunged into the river together. The current was strong and pushed at his legs, and the river rocks were round and slick. He slipped and fell to his knees and recovered. The water was surprisingly cold.

"Maybe Dietrich is pinned under the truck," Woods said. "I don't know."

The windshield glass was broken out of the cab when they got there, and Joe confirmed that Dietrich wasn't inside. The current flowed through the smashed-out rear window and through the open windshield. Anything inside would have been washed downstream.

Joe balanced himself against the crumpled metal

hood of the pickup and gazed down the river.

"There he is," Joe said. Twenty yards downstream, beneath the surface, Dietrich's overlarge jacket rippled underwater in the current. His body had been sucked under and was wedged in the river rocks. At a distance downstream where the river made a rightward bend, his large straw hat was caught at the base of some willows.

By the time they dragged the surprisingly light body to the bank, three more sheriff's department vehicles had arrived along with an ambulance. Sheriff Reed dispatched his men to take measurements and photographs of the bridge and the vehicles, and statements from Kyle Jr. and Sandra Hamburger.

Joe leaned against his pickup with a fleece blanket over his shoulders, next to Kyle Sr.

"Sheriff Reed hasn't said anything about any charges," Kyle Sr. said. "I don't know if he's gonna file on Sandra, or Kyle Junior, or neither. It was a damn accident, plain as day. Anybody can see that."

Joe nodded.

"That poor Sandra, you know how she is. If she's running late there isn't anything she'll let slow her down. I don't even know if she saw Kyle Junior coming across the bridge. I asked her but she just keeps blubbering about her schedule being screwed up."

Kyle Sr. sighed heavily. "That son of mine—I

hope he's okay after this. It's a hell of a thing that happened."

"Yup," Joe said, looking over at Kyle Jr. in the back of the SUV. When he did, the boy quickly looked away.

"I don't know what's going to happen now," Kyle Sr. said, nodding toward the ranch. "I don't know if he had heirs or what."

"Whatever happens will take awhile," Joe said. "You might as well hunker down and see where it goes."

"I guess."

"It might take years to straighten out," Joe said. "These things take time to sort out."

Kyle Sr. looked over and closed one eye. "What are you getting at, Joe?"

"Kyle Junior will be able to stick around. He might even graduate here."

"He'd like that."

"Yup," Joe said.

Later that night, after dinner, Joe told his wife, Marybeth, about the accident and the death. April listened in as well, and wondered aloud if Kyle would be in school on Monday.

After April left the table, Marybeth looked hard at Joe and said, "What's wrong? Something is bugging you."

He was astonished, as always, how she could read his mind.

He said, "I don't know for sure, I keep thinking about Kyle Junior. He's an observer, you know? He kind of hangs back and just tracks everything around him."

Marybeth nodded her head, then gestured for him to go on.

"He saw Sandra on her rounds on his way to the airport, just like I did," Joe said. "He knows her schedule. He knows the rhythm of that ranch and when Sandra Hamburger is going to show up every day. And he knows how she is. He also knew old man Dietrich didn't buckle his seat belt when he got in the truck."

Marybeth sat back and covered her mouth with her hand.

"Joe, are you saying . . ."

"I'm not saying *anything*. But it sure was unique timing for him to just happen to be on that bridge going one way when Sandra was on it coming the other, driving like her hair was on fire."

"My God," Marybeth whispered.

"No way to prove a thing," Joe said. "Not unless Kyle Junior decides to break down and confess, and no one is accusing him of anything. Heck, they might not even believe him if he did."

After a long pause, Marybeth asked, "Are you going to mention this to the sheriff?"

Joe shook his head. "Nope."

PIRATES OF
YELLOWSTONE

Vladdy pressed his forehead against the glass of the van window as they drove. The metal briefcase was on the floor, between his legs. It was cold in Yellowstone Park in early June, and dirty tongues of snow glowed light blue in the timber from the moonlight. The tires of the van hissed on the road.

"Look," Vladdy said to Eddie, gesturing out the window at the ghostly forms emerging in the meadow. "Elks."

"I see 'em every night," the driver said. "They like to eat the willows. And you don't say 'elks.' You say 'elk.' Like in, 'a herd of elk.'"

"My pardon," Vladdy said, self-conscious.

"You going to tell me what's in the briefcase?" the driver asked, smiling to show that he wasn't making a threat.

"No, I think not," Vladdy said.

The girl, Cherry, would be angry with him at first, Vladdy knew that. While she was at work at the motel that day, Vladdy had sold her good stereo and DVD unit to a man in a pawnshop full of rifles for $115, less $90 for a .22 pistol with a broken handgrip. But when she found out why he had done it, he was sure she would come around.

The whole thing was kind of her idea in the first place, after all.

The driver of the van was going from Mammoth Hot Springs in the northern part of the park to Cody, Wyoming, out the east entrance. He had told them he had to pick up some people at the Cody airport early in the morning and deliver them to a dude ranch. The driver was one of those middle-aged Americans who dressed and acted like it was 1968, Vladdy thought. The driver thought he was cool, giving a ride to Vladdy and Eddie, who obviously looked cold and out of place and carried a thick metal briefcase and nothing else. The driver had long curly hair on the side of his head with a huge mustache that was turning gray. He had agreed to give them a ride after they waved him down on the side of the road. The driver lit up a marijuana cigarette and offered it to them as he drove. Eddie accepted. Vladdy declined. He wanted to keep his head clear for what was going to happen when they crossed the huge park and came out through the tunnels and crossed the river. He had not done business in America yet, and he knew that Americans could be tough and ruthless in business. It was one of the qualities that had attracted Vladdy in the first place.

"Don't get too high," Vladdy told Eddie in Czech.

"I won't," Eddie said back. "I'm just a little scared, if that's all right with you. This helps."

"I wish you wouldn't wear that hat," Vladdy said. "You don't look professional."

"I look like Marshall Mathers, I think. Slim Shady," Eddie said, touching the stocking cap that was pulled over his eyebrows. He sounded a little hurt.

"Hey, dudes," the driver said over his shoulder to his passengers in the backseat, "speak American or I'm dropping you off on the side of the road. Deal?"

"Of course," Vladdy said. "We have deal."

Eddie was talking to the driver, talking too much, Vladdy thought. Eddie's English was very poor. It was embarrassing. Eddie was telling the driver about Prague, about the beautiful women there. The driver said he always wanted to go to Prague. Eddie tried to describe the buildings, but was doing a bad job of it.

"I don't care about buildings," the driver said. "Tell me about the women."

Vladimir and Eduard were branded "Vladdy" and "Eddie" by the man in the Human Resources office for Yellowstone in Gardiner, Montana, when they showed up to get their work assignment three weeks before and were told that there were no openings. Vladdy had explained that there must have been some kind of mix-up, some kind of misunderstanding, because they had been assured by the agent in Prague that both of them had been accepted to work for the official park concessionaire for the whole summer and into the fall. Vladdy showed the paperwork that allowed them to work on a visa for six months.

He had not yet seen the whole park, and it was something he very much wanted to do. He had read about the place since he was young, and watched Yellowstone documentaries on television. He knew there were three kinds of thermal activity: geysers, mudpots, and fumeroles. He knew there were over ten thousand places where the molten core of the earth broke through the thin crust. He knew that the park was the home of bison, elk, mountain sheep, and many fishes. People from all over the world came here to see it, smell it, feel it. Vladdy was still outside of it, though, looking in, like Yellowstone Park was still on a television show and not right in front of him. He wouldn't allow himself to become a part of this place yet. That would come later.

Yellowstone, like a microcosm of America, was a place of wonders, and it sought Eastern Europeans to work making beds, washing dishes, and cleaning out the muck from the trail horses, jobs that American workers didn't want or need. Many Czechs Vladdy and Eddie knew had come here, and some had stayed. It was good work in a fantastic place, "a setting from a dream of nature," as Vladdy put it. But the man in Human Resources had said he was sorry, they were overstaffed and there was nothing he could do until somebody quit and a couple of slots opened up. Even if that happened, the non-hiring man said, there were people on the list in front of them.

Vladdy had explained in his almost-perfect English, he thought, that he and Eddie didn't have the money to go back. In fact, he told the man, they didn't even have the money for a room to wait in. What they had was on their backs— cracked black leather jackets, ill-fitting clothes, street shoes. Eddie wore the stocking cap because he liked Eminem, but Vladdy preferred his slicked-back-hair look. They looked nothing like the other young people their age they saw in the office and on the streets.

"Keep in touch," the hiring man had told Vladdy. "Check back every few days."

"I can't even buy cigarettes," Vladdy had pleaded.

The man felt sorry for them and gave them a $20 bill out of his own wallet.

"I told you we should have gone to Detroit," Eddie said to Vladdy in Czech.

Vladdy and Eddie had spent that first unhappy day after meeting the non-hiring man in a place called K-Bar Pizza in Gardiner, Montana. They sat at a round table, and were so close to the Human Resources building that when the door to the K-Bar opened they could see it out there. Vladdy had placed the $20 on the table and ordered two tap beers, which they both agreed were awful. Then they ordered a Budweiser, which was nothing like the Czechoslovakian Budweiser, and they laughed about that. Cherry was their waitress. She told Vladdy she was from Kansas, someplace like that. He could tell she was uncomfortable with herself, with her appearance, because she was a little fat and had a crooked face. She told Vladdy she was divorced, with a kid, and she worked at the K-Bar to supplement her income. She also had a job at a motel, servicing rooms. He could tell she was flattered by his attention, by his leather jacket, his hair, his smile, his accent. Sometimes women reacted this way to him, and he appreciated it. He hadn't known if his looks would work for him in America, and he still didn't know. But they worked in Gardiner, Montana. Vladdy knew he had found a friend when she let them keep ordering even though the $20 was spent, and she didn't discourage them from staying until her shift was over.

Cherry led them down the steep, cracked sidewalks and through an alley to an old building backed up to the edge of a canyon. Vladdy looked around as he followed. He didn't understand Gardiner. In every direction he looked, he could only see space. Mountains, bare hillsides, an empty valley going north, under the biggest sky he had ever seen. Yet Gardiner was packed together. Houses almost touched houses, windows opened up to other windows. It was like a tiny island in an ocean of . . . nothing. Vladdy decided he would find out about this.

She made them stand in the hallway while she went in to check to make sure her little boy was in bed, then she let them sleep in the front room of her two-bedroom apartment. That first night, Vladdy waited until Eddie was snoring and then he padded across the linoleum floor in his bare feet and opened Cherry's bedroom door. She was pretending she was asleep, and he said nothing, just stood there in his underwear.

"What do you want?" Cherry asked him sleepily.

"I want to pleasure you," he whispered.

"Don't turn on the light," she said. "I don't want you to look at me."

Afterward, in the dark, Vladdy could hear the furious river below them in the canyon. It sounded so raw, like an angry young river trying to figure out what it wanted to be when it grew up.

While Eddie and Vladdy checked back with the non-hiring man every morning, Vladdy tried to help out around the house since he had no money for rent. He tried to fix the dripping faucet, but couldn't find any tools in the apartment besides an old pair of pliers and something cheap designed to slice potatoes. He mopped the floors, though, and washed her windows. He fixed her leaking toilet with the pliers. While he did this, Eddie sat on the couch and watched television, MTV mostly. Cherry's kid, Tony, sat with Eddie and watched and wouldn't even change out of his pajamas and get dressed unless Vladdy told him to do so.

Vladdy was taking the garbage out to the dumpster when he first saw Cherry's neighbor, a man whose name he later learned was Bob. Vladdy thought it was funny, and very American, to have a one-syllable name like "Bob." It made him laugh inside.

Bob pulled up to the building in a dark, massive four-wheel-drive car. The car was mud-splashed, scratched, and dented, even though it didn't look very old. It was a huge car, and Vladdy recognized it as a Suburban. Vladdy watched as Bob came out of the car. Bob had a hard, impatient look on his face. He wore dirty blue jeans, a sweatshirt, a fleece vest, and a baseball cap, like everyone else in Gardiner.

Bob stepped away from the back of the Suburban, slammed both doors, and locked it with a remote. That's when Vladdy first saw the metal briefcase. It was the briefcase Bob was retrieving from the back of the Suburban.

And with that, Bob went into the building.

• • •

That night, after Eddie and Tony had gone out to bring back fried chicken from the deli at the grocery store for dinner, Vladdy asked Cherry about her neighbor Bob. He described the metal briefcase.

"I'd stay away from him, if I was you," Cherry said. "I've got my suspicions about that Bob."

Vladdy was confused.

"I hear things at the K-Bar," Cherry said. "I seen him in there a couple of times by himself. He's not the friendliest guy I've ever met."

"He's not like me," Vladdy said, reaching across the table and brushing a strand of her hair out of her eyes.

Cherry sat back in the chair and studied Vladdy. "No, he's not like you," she said.

After pleasuring Cherry, Vladdy waited until she was asleep before he crept through the dark front room where Eddie was sleeping. Vladdy found a flashlight in a drawer in the kitchen and slipped outside into the hallway. He went down the stairs in his underwear, went outside, and approached the back of the Suburban.

Turning on the flashlight, he saw rumpled clothing, rolls of maps, hiking boots, and electrical equipment with dials and gauges. He noticed a square of open carpet where the metal briefcase sat when Bob wasn't carrying it around.

He wondered if Bob wasn't an engineer, or a scientist of some kind. He wondered where it was that Bob went every day to do his work, and what he kept in the metal briefcase that couldn't be left with the rest of his things.

Vladdy had taken classes in geology and geography and chemistry. He had done well in them, and he wondered if maybe Bob needed some help, needed an assistant. At least until a job opened up in the park.

Cherry surprised them by bringing two bottles of Jack Daniel's home after her shift at the K-Bar, and they had whiskey on ice while they ate Lean Cuisine dinners. They kept drinking afterward at the table. Vladdy suspected that Cherry had stolen the bottles from behind the bar, but said nothing because he was enjoying himself and he wanted to ask her about Bob. Eddie was getting pretty drunk, and was telling funny stories in Czech that Cherry and Tony didn't understand. But the way he told them made everyone laugh. Tony said he wanted a drink, too, and Eddie started to pour him one until Vladdy told Eddie not to do it. Eddie took his own drink to the couch, sulking, the evening ruined for him, he said.

"Cherry," Vladdy said, "I feel bad inside that I cannot pay rent."

Cherry waved him off. "You pay the rent in

other ways," she laughed. "My floor and windows have never been cleaner. Not to mention your other . . . services."

Vladdy looked over his shoulder to make sure Tony hadn't heard his mother.

"I am serious," Vladdy said, trying to make her look him in the eye. "I'm a serious man. Because I don't have a job yet, I want to work. I wonder maybe if your neighbor Bob needs an apprentice in his work. Somebody who would get mud on himself if Bob doesn't want to."

Cherry shook her head and smiled, and took a long time to answer. She searched Vladdy's face for something that Vladdy hoped his face had. When she finally spoke, her voice was low for a change. She leaned her head forward, toward Vladdy.

"I told you I've heard some things about Bob at the K-Bar," she said softly. "I heard that Bob is a bio pirate. He's a criminal."

"What is this bio pirate?"

He could smell her whiskey breath, but he bent closer.

"In Yellowstone, in some of the hot pots and geysers, there are rare microorganisms that can only be found here. Our government is studying some of them legitimately, trying to find out if they could be a cure for cancer, or maybe a bioweapon, or whatever. It's illegal to take them out of the park. But the rumor is there are some people stealing the microbes and selling them. You know, bio pirates."

Vladdy sat back for a moment to think. Her eyes burned into his as they never had before. It was the whiskey, sure, but it was something else.

"The metal briefcase," Vladdy whispered. "That's where he keeps the microbes."

Cherry nodded enthusiastically. "Who knows what they're worth? Or better yet, who knows what someone would pay us to give them back and not say anything about it?"

Vladdy felt a double-edged chill, of both excitement and fear. This Cherry, he thought, she didn't just come up with this. She had been thinking about it for a while.

"Next time he's at the K-Bar, I'll call you," she said. "He doesn't bring his briefcase with him there. He keeps it next door, in his apartment, when he goes out at night. That's where it will be when I call you."

"Hey," Tony called from the couch, "what are you two whispering about over there?"

"They talk *fornication,*" Eddie said with a slur, making Tony laugh. As far as Vladdy knew, it was Eddie's first American sentence.

Vladdy was wiping the counter clean with Listerine—he loved Listerine, and thought it was the best disinfectant in the entire world—when the telephone rang. A bolt shot up his spine. He looked around. Eddie and Tony were watching television.

It was Cherry. "He's here at the K-Bar, and he ordered a pitcher just for himself. He's settling in for a while."

"Settling in?" Vladdy asked, not understanding.

"Jesus," she said. "I mean he'll be here for a while. Which means his briefcase is in his apartment. Come on, Vladdy."

"I understand," Vladdy said.

"Get over there," Cherry said. "I love you."

Vladdy had thought about this, the fact that he didn't love Cherry. He liked her, he appreciated her kindness, he felt obligated to her, but he didn't love her at all. So he used a phrase he had heard in the grocery store.

"You bet," he said.

Hanging up, he asked Eddie to take Tony to the grocery store and get him some ice cream. Eddie winked at Vladdy as they left, because Vladdy had told Eddie about the bio pirates.

The metal briefcase wasn't hard to find, and it was much easier than shinnying along a two-inch ridge of brick outside the window in his shiny street shoes with the mad river roaring somewhere in the dark beneath him. He was happy that Bob's outside window slid open easily, and he stepped through the open window into Bob's kitchen sink, cracking a dirty plate with his heel.

It made some sense that the metal case was in the refrigerator, on a large shelf of its own, and he pulled it out by the handle, which was cold.

Back in Cherry's apartment, he realized he was still shivering, and it wasn't from the temperature outside. But he opened the briefcase on the kitchen table. Yes, there were glass vials filled with murky water. Cherry was right. And in the inside of the top of the briefcase was a taped business card. There was Bob's name and a cell phone number on the business card.

Vladdy poured the last of the Jack Daniel's Cherry had stolen into a water glass and drank most of it. He waited until the burn developed in his throat before he dialed.

"What?" Bob answered. Vladdy pictured Bob sitting at a table in the K-Bar. He wondered if Cherry was watching.

"I have an important briefcase, full of water samples," Vladdy said, trying to keep his voice deep and level. "I found it in your flat."

"Who in the hell are *you?* How did you get my number?"

Vladdy remembered a line from an American movie he saw at home. "I am your worst nightmare," he said. It felt good to say it.

"Where are you from that you talk like that?" Bob asked. "How in the hell did you get into my apartment?"

Vladdy didn't answer. He didn't know what to say.

"Damn it," Bob said. "What do you want?"

Vladdy breathed deeply, tried to stay calm. "I want two thousand dollars for your metal briefcase, and I won't say a word about it to anyone."

"Two thousand?" Bob said in a dismissive way that instantly made Vladdy wish he had asked for ten thousand, or twenty thousand. "I don't have that much cash on me. I'll have to get it in Cody tomorrow, at my bank."

"Yes, that would be fine," Vladdy said.

Silence. Thinking. Vladdy could hear something in the background, probably the television above the bar.

"Okay," Bob said. "Meet me tomorrow night at eleven p.m. on the turnout after the tunnels on the Buffalo Bill Dam. East entrance, on the way to Cody. Don't bring anybody with you, and don't tell anyone about this conversation. If you do, I'll know."

Vladdy felt an icy hand reach down his throat and grip his bowels. This was real, after all. This was American business, and he was committed. *Stay tough,* he told himself.

"I have a partner," Vladdy said. "He comes with me."

More silence. Then a sigh. "Only him," the man said. "No one else."

"Okay."

"I'll be in a dark Suburban, parked in the turnout."

"Okay." Vladdy knew the vehicle, of course, but he couldn't give that away.

"If you show up with more than your partner, or if there are any other vehicles on the road, this deal is over. And I mean over in the worst possible sense. You understand?"

Vladdy paused, and the telephone nearly slipped out of his sweaty hand like a bar of soap.

"Okay," Vladdy said. When he hung up the telephone, it rattled so hard in the cradle from his hand that it took him two tries.

Vladdy and Eddie sat in silence on the couch and listened as Bob crashed around in his apartment next door. Had Vladdy left any clues? he wondered. Would Bob notice the cracked plate in the sink and determine Vladdy's entry method?

Eddie looked scared. After an hour, the crashing stopped. Vladdy and Eddie watched Cherry's door, praying that Bob wouldn't realize they were there and smash through it.

"I think we're okay," Vladdy said finally. "He doesn't know who took it."

Vladdy kept his cheek pressed against the cold window as they left Yellowstone Park. He closed his eyes temporarily as the van rumbled through the east entrance, and noted the sign that read ENTERING SHOSHONE NATIONAL FOREST.

Eddie was still talking, still smoking. He had long ago worked his way into the front so that he sat next to the driver. A second marijuana cigarette had been passed back and forth. The driver was talking about democracy versus socialism, and was for the latter. Vladdy thought the driver was an idiot, an idiot who pined for a forgotten political system that had never, ever worked, and a system that Vladdy despised. But Vladdy said nothing, because Eddie wouldn't stop talking, wouldn't quit agreeing with the driver.

They went through three tunnels, lit by orange ambient light, and Vladdy stared through the glass. The Shoshone River serpentined below them, reflecting the moonlight. They crossed it on a bridge.

"Let us off here," Vladdy said as they cleared the last tunnel and the reservoir sparkled beneath the moon and starlight to the right as far as he could see.

The driver slowed, then turned around in his seat. "Are you sure?" he asked. "There's nothing out here except for the dam. It's another half hour to Cody and not much in between."

"This is our place," Vladdy said. "Thank you for the drive."

The van braked, and stopped.

"Are you sure?" the driver asked.

"Pay him, Eddie," Vladdy said, sliding across the seat toward the door with the metal briefcase. He listened vaguely as the driver insisted he needed no payment and as Eddie tried to stuff a twenty in the driver's pocket. Which he did, eventually, and the van pulled away en route to Cody, which was a cream-colored smudge in the distance, like an inverted half-moon against the dark eastern sky.

"What now?" Eddie asked, and Vladdy and Eddie walked along the dark shoulder of the road, crunching gravel beneath their shoes.

"Now?" Vladdy said in English. "I don't know. You've got the gun in your pants, right? You may need to use it as a threat. You've got it, right?"

Eddie did a hitch in his step as he dug through his coat.

"I got it, Vladdy," Eddie said. "But is small. What if it don't even shoot?"

Vladdy's teeth began to chatter as they approached the turnout and he saw the Suburban. The vehicle was parked on the far side of the lot, backed up against the railing of the dam. The car was dark.

"Are you scared?" Eddie asked. He was still high.

"Just cold," Vladdy lied.

Vladdy's legs felt weak, and he concentrated on walking forward toward the big car.

Vladdy said, "Don't smile at him. Look tough."

"Tough," Eddie repeated.

Vladdy said to Eddie, "I told you to look professional, but you look like Eminem."

"Slim Shady is my *man,*" Eddie whined.

At twenty yards, the headlights blinded them. Vladdy put his arm up to shield his eyes. Then the headlights went out and he heard a car door open and slam shut. He couldn't see anything now but the orange and blue afterimage of the headlights. He heard fast-moving footfalls coming across the gravel.

Vladdy's eyes readjusted to the darkness in time to see Bob raise a pistol and shoot Eddie point-blank in the forehead, right through his stocking cap. Eddie dropped straight down as if his legs had been kicked out from under him, and he landed in a heap.

"Some fuckin' nightmare," Bob said, pointing the pistol at Vladdy. "Where are you boys *from?*"

Instinctively, Vladdy fell back. As he did so, he raised the metal briefcase and felt a shock through his hand and arm as a bullet smashed into it. On the ground, Vladdy heard a cry and realized that it had come from inside of him. He thrashed and rolled away, and Bob cursed and fired another booming shot into the dirt near Vladdy's ear.

Vladdy leaped forward and swung the briefcase as wildly as he could, and by pure chance it hit hard into Bob's kneecaps. Bob grunted and pitched forward, nearly onto Vladdy. In the dark, Vladdy had no idea where Bob's gun was, but he scrambled to his feet and clubbed at Bob with the briefcase.

Bob said, "Stop!" but all Vladdy could see was the muzzle flash on Eddie's face a moment before.

"Stop! I've got the—" Vladdy smashed the briefcase down as hard as he could and stopped the sentence. Bob lay still.

Breathing hard, Vladdy dropped the briefcase and fell on top of Bob. He tore through Bob's clothing and found the gun that shot Eddie. Bob moaned, and Vladdy shot him in the eye with it.

With tears streaming down his face, Vladdy buckled Eddie's and Bob's belts together and rolled them off the dam. He heard the bodies thump into some rocks and then splash into the reservoir. He threw the pistol as far as he could and it went into the water with a *ploop*. The briefcase followed.

He found a vinyl bag on the front seat of the Suburban that bulged with $2,000 in cash. It puzzled Vladdy for a moment, but then it made sense. Bob had flashed his lights to see who had taken his briefcase. When he saw two out-of-place guys like Vladdy and Eddie—*especially* Eddie— Bob made his choice not to pay.

∙ ∙

Vladdy drove back through Yellowstone Park in the Suburban, thinking of Eddie, thinking of what he had done. He would buy some new clothes, new shoes, one of those fleece vests. Get a baseball cap, maybe.

He parked on a turnout on the northern shore of Yellowstone Lake and watched the sun come up. Steam rose from hot spots along the bank, and a V of Canada geese made a long, graceful descent onto the surface of the water.

He felt a part of it, now.

A setting from a dream of nature, he thought.

THE END OF
JIM AND EZRA

The Wind River Range
Wyoming Territory, 1835

It took great determination for Jim—almost more than he had left inside him—not to throw back the heavy buffalo robes and slice Ezra's throat open. His sheathed bowie knife was in his bed within easy reach, where it had been each night for the past twenty-eight years. Jim clamped his eyes shut and stroked the leather-wrapped handle with his fingertips. The blade was as sharp and as long as his thigh and he had used it to cut apart hundreds of buffalo, elk, deer, and bears. It had skinned a thousand beaver and he had shaved with it back when he shaved, and it had pierced the insides of three Indian bucks; two Arikara and a Pawnee. But he'd never used it to kill a friend.

Jim felt ashamed and he opened his hand beneath the robes and released the knife handle.

It was freezing inside the cabin, as it had been every morning for six weeks. The cold had made the chinking between the logs contract, crack, and fall out in chunks. The series of gaps let wind blow through the walls and a half-dozen inch-high snowdrifts had formed across the top of his robes, striping them, making them look, as Ezra pointed out each and every morning, as if he were sleeping under a zebra hide. Ice crystals tipped the ends of individual hairs on the outside of the robe as well. Making it as gray as Jim's beard.

He fought against the urge to grasp the knife again as Ezra's socked feet thumped the rough wood-plank floor. Jim listened in tortured silence as Ezra rose unsteadily to full height and stretched. Ezra's bones cracked like ice shifting on a lake, a combination of low-grounded pops and high snapping sounds. Ezra growled from deep in his chest and worked a gob of phlegm up into the back of his throat while he sniffed in the fluid of his nose so it could all mix together into a substantial globule he called his "morning mass" because he was Catholic. Ezra just held it there—sometimes it seemed for a half an hour to Jim—while the man poked and prodded the fire and added lengths of split wood until it took off and started to roar. Waiting for the flames, Ezra breathed raggedly through his nose because his mouth was full. When the fire was intense enough that the metal grate was hot, Ezra spit his morning mass onto the bars of the grate and said, "Lookit that thang burn."

Sometimes, Jim could hear it pop.

Jim knew Ezra would then say, "Jim, come lookit this thang," because Ezra said it each and every morning, and had for ninety-two straight days. He said it again.

Ninety-three.

Ezra turned stiffly toward Jim while he pulled a clawed hand down through his matted beard to groom it. He'd once stood six-foot-four before he got that hump in his back and his legs bowed out as wide as his shoulders. He'd worn the union suit so long his leg hairs were growing out through the fabric. White salty blooms framed the crotch. A tobacco stain looked like a permanent teardrop under his left breast. Both elbows of the suit had long since worn away and Ezra's blue-white joints stuck out the holes.

He cackled and said to Jim, "Lookit you sleeping under that zebra hide! It looks like a damn zebra hide the way it's all striped like that."

The cabin, corral, fur shack, and loafing shed had been thrown together on the western side of the Wind River Mountains too high up and too far from anyone or anything else. They'd been caught in early September by snow, and Jim could tell by just looking at the sky that more was coming fast, that it was just the beginning of a mean and heartless winter.

They'd been trapped by their own success, a phrase Ezra had latched onto and repeated two or three times a day.

It had been Jim's idea, born of frustration and lack of beaver in the lowland creeks and streams, to go higher and farther into the mountains than they'd ever gone before. Farther than *any* white trappers had gone before. There'd been a sense of urgency because they were being pushed by newcomers. More of them all the time, flowing west and north across the continent like a plague. The newcomers had no idea how rough and raggedy it had once been, and had little appreciation for men like Jim and Ezra, who had scouted the rivers and valleys and found the beaver and fought the Indians. Jim and Ezra were like the elk. Once plains animals, they'd been pressured to seek higher ground.

It wasn't fair, but Jim had never thought fairness was his due. So many things were working against them. The scarcity of beaver. The discovery back east that silk worked better for top hats than beaver felt. The plummeting price of beaver plews (pelts). And their aged and aching bodies.

Three things bound them together, two being their history and their treasure.

The third thing was the fact they were snowbound nine thousand feet in the mountains.

And all Jim could think of these days was how much he wanted to kill Ezra.

The fur shack outside bulged with skinned beaver plews six feet high by eight feet deep. The plews had been stretched and bound together. Now they were frozen into bales so heavy it took two men to load them. They were worth a fortune.

The cabin was one room, roughly twenty by twenty feet. There were two frame beds cross-hatched with rope to provide some give, a table that listed to the right, two chairs, a slab-rock fireplace that wasn't tight, and no windows except for the four-inch square in the door covered with bear-greased cotton cloth. Every corner of the structure was filled with snarls of traps and chains. They had one pot, one frying pan, and a tin for coffee and hot water.

It had been over three months.

They'd nearly made up for all of the things working against them the previous fall. They trapped more beaver—hundreds of them—than they ever had before as they worked their way up the river to its source.

They called the place Green River Lake and it was magnificent: a huge body of water over-looked by a square-topped granite tower that seemed carved to resemble the massive turret of a German or French castle. Not that either of them had seen a castle, but Ezra had a book with a picture in it. The inlets to the lake teemed with beaver and the lake itself was brimming with plump cutthroat trout.

And once they found the beaver, Jim wouldn't stop. He urged Ezra to stay, until the two of them could barely walk due to their arthritic knees made worse by standing thigh-high in freezing water day after day checking their traps. Jim didn't say "That's enough" until they had to break through skins of ice to get to the drowned beavers.

By then it was too late. Winter was setting in. The logistics of transporting their bales of skinned beaver plews to Fort Bridger—it would have taken two trips—were impossible. Plus, they couldn't leave their treasure or cache it. Indians would find it and steal it and sell off their year's work. The Indians wouldn't even consider it stealing. They'd consider it "finding." Jim understood that and didn't hate the Indians for the way they thought. They were well aware of the waves of newcomers. And they needed money and guns, too.

So Jim and Ezra built a temporary shelter, until the weather broke. But it never did.

Breakfast was fatty beaver tail and the last half of a ptarmigan Jim had shot the day before. The ptarmigan was delicious. Jim watched Ezra eat. Ezra chewed loudly and smacked his lips and his pointy tongue shot out of his mouth to catch droplets of grease on the tips of his mustache. When the bird was stripped of flesh, Ezra snapped off every bone and sucked the marrow dry until the bones were no more than translucent tubes on his plate.

Ezra said, "I'd give my left nut for coffee."

Jim said, "Might as well. You got no other use for it anymore."

A gust of wind hit the north wall of the cabin and shot a spray of snow inside.

"Wished I'd done a better job of chinking," Ezra said.

"Me too."

"Got any ideas how we can fix it? Mine wasn't so good."

Jim said nothing. It had been Ezra's suggestion to fill the gaps with bear fat, thinking that the fat would freeze and seal hard as plaster. It worked for a week, until the grizzlies found it and licked it clean. One night, Jim and Ezra sat on Ezra's bed with their .50 Hawken rifles across their knees, hoping the bears didn't push the cabin down around them. They watched as huge wet pink tongues flicked between the logs. They could hear the bears smacking their lips and clicking their three-inch teeth. Jim went nearly mad from fear and impatience and finally went outside and shot a sow to warn them off, but the bears came back that night and licked the rest of the fat clean and tried to smash down the door. Jim and Ezra ate the sow.

"It's gotta stop one of these days," Ezra said, and paused. "The storms."

"It's winter."

"We're trapped by our own success."

Jim closed his eyes. He *knew* he'd hear that again.

Jim blew into the cabin from outside with gouts of swirling snow. Ezra looked up from where he sat at the table shaving curls of meat from a frozen deer haunch into the pot for stew. "You look like a damned snow bear," he said. Ezra was always *observing* him, Jim thought. And he never kept his observations to himself.

Jim had to use his shoulder to close the door against the wind and he slid the timber across the braces to seal it shut. He shook snow from his buffalo coat and hung it on a peg. His leggings were wet and packed with snow, and his winter knee-high moccasins needed to be greased because his feet were wet. The snow was six feet deep outside, more than halfway up the cabin. Paths outside the front door—rimmed by vertical walls of snow—led to the corral, the fur house, and to where the outhouse had been before it got buried. Yellow and brown stains spotted the top of the snow but they lasted only until the next storm. Ezra had stopped going outside several weeks before and had been using a leaky chamber pot he'd fashioned himself from pine staves. It was nearly full. He set it just outside the door each night so it would freeze solid. Unfortunately, he brought it back inside during the day.

Jim said, "Emily's dead."

Ezra shook his head. "How?"

"Froze to death. Hard as a rock. Must have happened last night."

"Wolves get to her?"

"Not that I could see."

"Is she too froze to quarter?"

"Ezra," Jim said, "I ain't eating Emily. She was a good horse. I ain't eating her."

Ezra shrugged. "What's dead is just meat, Jim. You know that. You ate horses before."

"We *had* to," Jim said. "We had nothing else."

"Just thought you'd like something new for a change."

"Not horse. Horse reminds me of Birdwing and all that happened."

The first winter, after they'd gone all the way to the other ocean with Colonel Ashley's merchant party and turned around and struck out on their own to become trappers, Jim had taken a wife. A pretty Crow named Birdwing. While Jim and Ezra were out scouting creeks, the Pawnee broke into Jim's cabin on the Bighorn River and took her. Jim and Ezra pursued the Pawnee for a month and found them and killed them all, only to find out Birdwing had died of disease the week before. On their way back, with Jim mourning and not speaking for days, the Pawnee found *them*. The bucks killed their pack horses and chased them into the badlands, where they literally rode their good horses to death in order to escape. And ate them.

"Birdwing," Ezra said, after about five minutes of shaving meat into their pot. "You still think about her."

Jim grunted.

"I think about that little whore at Fort Laramie," Ezra said, smiling manically. "The redhead. I think about her every night before I go to sleep."

Jim took a deep breath and said, "I know. I'm only ten feet away from you."

Ezra guffawed. He'd never been contrite about that. Even when he worked himself so furiously he sometimes fell out of his bed.

"All I know," Ezra said, "is this is the last of our fresh meat. Unless you can kill us something real soon, Emily might start looking pretty good out there."

"I ain't eating Emily," Jim growled. "She was a good horse."

"And now," Ezra said, "we're plumb out of horses."

"We can get some come spring," Jim said. "We can trade some plews for 'em if we have to."

"Never should have come up this far," Ezra said, shaking his head.

Jim turned away, his rage building.

"Sorry," Ezra said, "I shouldn't have said that."

"You could have left any damned time," Jim said through clenched teeth. "I wouldn't have stopped you."

Three months and Ezra hadn't said it, Jim thought. Three months Ezra had held it in.

"After all we been through together?" Ezra said.

That night they ate deer meat boiled in melted snow and didn't say one word to each other. The wind sliced through the cabin and the tallow candle shimmered and blew out. They finished eating in the dark. Jim kept waiting for Ezra to light the candle again because he had the matches. Ezra just ate, and sucked on his mustache and beard for dessert.

Jim didn't have to watch to know what he was doing. He knew the sound. He smoldered.

After Ezra was done with the whore from Fort Laramie, Jim said, "Don't forget, our fortune is right outside. I'm sure you want your half when this is all said and done."

Since they'd been holed up, there had been an unspoken rule that they didn't talk after they went to bed. Too intimate. Jim had broken protocol, but he was still seething.

"I said I was sorry for sayin' that, Jim. Just forget it."

"You could have left anytime. We could have squared up and you could have left."

Ezra said, "It's a cold one tonight."

"You can leave tomorrow if you want," Jim said. "I'll get those plews down myself and I'll sell 'em and send you your share wherever the hell you wind up. Just leave word at the fort where you want the money sent."

Ezra sighed. "You're like a dog with a rag in its mouth, Jim. You won't let go."

Jim closed his hand around his knife, and went to sleep that way.

Lines of snow, like jail bars, formed across the top of his blankets.

The next morning, Jim kept his eyes closed and gripped the handle of his knife while Ezra coughed himself awake, hacked phlegm into a ball in his mouth, and got the fire going.

Ezra spit the gob onto the grate and said, "Lookit that thang burn. Jim, come lookit this thang."

Jim threw his covers aside, sat up, said through gritted teeth, "I'm leaving. I'll be back come spring."

Ezra stroked his beard and squinted at Jim. "How you going to cover two hundred miles in the snow to get to Fort Bridger?"

Jim gathered and tied up his ropes as a backpack and filled a leather sack with half the pemmican. He grabbed his possibles sack from a peg and stuffed it with half their powder and lead.

"Take more if you want," Ezra said.

"This is fine. I'll manage." Jim couldn't even look at Ezra. He couldn't look at his rheumy eyes or filthy union suit or scraggly beard because he knew if he did he'd kill the man right there. Gut him, and toss the carcass outside for the grizzlies.

"The only way down is through the Pawnee winter camp," Ezra said. "They might not like that."

"Ezra," Jim said, hands shaking, "get out of my way."

"You want breakfast first?"

"Ezra, get out of my way."

"Just because I spit in the fire?"

"That and every other damned thing."

Ezra stepped back as if slapped.

As Jim pulled on his buffalo coat and clamped his red fox hat over his head, he heard Ezra say to his back, "God be with you in your travels, Jim. I'm going to miss you, my friend. We had some mighty great years together."

Jim plunged outside with his eyes stinging. He convinced himself it was due to the blowing needles of snow in his face.

Through the howling wind he thought he heard Ezra's voice, and he turned.

The wind whipped Ezra's words away, but Jim could read his lips. Ezra said, "We're victims of our . . ."

Jim ignored the rest.

● ● ●

The Pawnee winter camp was massive, stretching the length and width of the river valley. There were lodges as far as Jim could see on both banks of the frozen river. Smoke hung low over the lodges, beaten down by the cold. Hundreds of ponies milled in corrals and Jim could hear packs of dogs yelp and bark. Because of the snow and cold he rarely saw a Pawnee venture outside their tipis and when they did it was a quick trip, either to get more wood, water from a chopped square in the ice, or to defecate in the skeletal buck brush.

From where he hunkered down in the deep powder snow on the top of a hillock, Jim tried to plot a way he could avoid the encampment and continue his trek. It had been four days and he'd eaten nothing but pemmican—meat, fat, and berries mushed together into frozen patties—and he was practically out of food. He'd found no game since he left the cabin, not even a snowshoe hare. He'd tried to eat the skin-like underbark of cottonwood and mountain ash trees like elk did, but the taste was acrid and it gave him no energy. A cold breeze from the valley floor brought whiffs of broiled meat, puppy probably, and his mouth salivated and his stomach growled.

He knew from his years in the mountains he was a few days away from death. He had no horse, no food, and he hadn't been able to feel his toes for twenty-four hours.

And he cursed Ezra once again and thought of going back. But he knew if he did, Ezra would have to die, because he couldn't spend another minute in the man's presence. Ezra had always been just a hair over the line into civilization and it hadn't taken him long to slip back and become an animal again. A filthy pig. Jim wondered why he hadn't seen it before, how close Ezra was to comfortable savagery. He imagined Ezra back in the cabin, eating his own leg.

It would be nightfall soon. The winter camp would go to sleep. If he could find their cache of meat, and steal a horse . . .

It took a long time to get back to the cabin. Jim didn't know for sure how many days and nights, but he guessed it was over a week. Most of the time, his head had been elsewhere, for hours at a time, and he sang and chanted and cursed the world and God and those Pawnees who had filled him full of arrows and murdered him for sure.

He lurched from tree to tree on columns of frozen rock that had once been his legs and he peered out at the pure white of the sky and the ground through his left eye because his right was blind. Somewhere along the way he'd lost his rifle and his possibles sack. He thought his knives were still in their sheaths under his buffalo coat, but he couldn't be sure and he didn't look.

Jim scooped up snow and ate it as if it were

food and it kept his tongue from swelling and cracking. He'd fallen on a snowshoe hare that was still warm from being killed by a bobcat and he pulled what was left of it apart and ate it raw.

He thanked God it hadn't snowed hard since he'd left, because he could follow his own trail back most of the way.

And he thanked Ezra when at last he smelled woodsmoke and meat cooking and there was the cabin, and the fur shack, and the corrals.

Jim wept as he approached the front door and pounded on it.

"Who is it?" Ezra asked from inside.

Jim couldn't speak. He sunk to his knees and thumped the door with the crown of his head.

The door opened and Jim fell inside. For the first time since he'd left, he felt warmth on his face.

And Ezra said, "You don't look so good, Jim."

Through the violent, roaring, excruciating pain that came from his frostbitten skin thawing out, Jim had crazy dreams. He dreamed Ezra had shaved, bathed, and put on clean clothes. He dreamed Ezra had re-chinked the logs and fireplace until they were tight with mud and straw and had emptied his chamber pot, swept the floor, and put the cabin in order. He dreamed Ezra awakened without hacking or spitting or even talking.

He thought, *I'm in heaven.*

But he wasn't.

Jim painfully rolled his head to the side. Ezra was sitting at the table, finishing his lunch of roast Emily. Ezra's face was shaved smooth and freshly scrubbed. His movements were spry and purposeful. His eyes were clear and blue.

Ezra said, "I didn't think you'd come back. I thought you'd make it to Fort Bridger because you're just so goddamned stubborn."

Jim couldn't speak. The pain came in crippling waves.

"I got the arrows out, but your flesh is rotten, Jim," Ezra said. "You know what that means."

Jim knew. He closed his eyes. The pain reached a crescendo and suddenly stopped. Just stopped.

Ezra's voice rose and was filled with emotion. "You ain't exactly the easiest man to live with, neither," he said.

And with that, Jim died, a victim of his success.

THE MASTER
FALCONER

In the midnight forests of the Bighorn Mountains, below timberline, all movement and sound ceased with the approaching roar. Elk quit grazing and raised their heads. Squirrels stopped chattering. The increasing roar caused the ground to tremble. And suddenly the stars blacked out as the huge aircraft skirted over the mountaintops, landing lights blazing, landing gear descending, the howl of jet engines pounding downward through the branches into the earth itself. The tiny town of Saddlestring, Wyoming, was laid out before the nose of the plane like a dropped jewelry box, lights winking in the night against black felt, the lighted runway just long enough for a plane this size to land on, but just barely.

The next morning, Nate Romanowski slipped out of Alisha Whiteplume's quilt-covered bed on the Wind River Indian Reservation, pulled on a loose pair of shorts, and searched through the cupboards of her small kitchen for coffee. He tried not to wake her. There were cans of refried beans and jars of picante sauce, home-canned trout in Mason jars, but no coffee except instant.

As two mugs of water heated in the microwave, he opened the kitchen blinds. Dawn. Early fall.

Dew and fallen leaves on the grass, dried into fists. A skinned-out antelope buck hung to cool from the basketball hoop over the garage.

Nate was tall, rangy, with sharp features and a deliberate, liquid way of moving. His expression was impassive, but his pale blue eyes flicked about from the hollows of his sockets like the tongue of a snake. Sometimes they fixed on an object and forgot to blink. Alisha said he had the eyes of a hunter.

"What are you doing out there?" she said from the dark of the bedroom.

"Heating water for coffee. Want anything in it?"

"Not instant. There's a can of coffee under the sink in the bathroom."

Nate started to ask why she kept coffee in the bathroom, but didn't.

"Bobby has been coming over in the morning and stealing it," she said in explanation. Bobby was Alisha's brother, known to Nate as Bad Bob. "I hid it so he has to go steal it from someone else."

Nate found a five-pound can of Folgers under the sink, and set about making a pot.

While it dripped and the aroma filled the kitchen, she came out of the bedroom wrapped in a blanket so long it brushed the floor. He glimpsed her thin brown feet and painted nails, and looked up to see her naked shoulder, a valentine-shaped face, bed-mussed black hair. Her eyes were obsidian pebbles perched over her cheekbones. He had yet to tire of simply looking at her.

"Did you hear that big plane last night?" she asked.

"I heard a roar. I thought it was me."

She smiled. "You did roar, but earlier. You were sleeping when the plane came over us. It seemed really low. I felt you tense up when it came over, like you were going to jump out of bed and grab a gun."

Nate didn't respond. She padded over and put her hand on his shoulder.

"Do you know who is in the plane?"

He shrugged and said, "I've got an idea."

"Are you going to say?"

"No, not yet."

"You drive me crazy," she said.

"You drive me wild," he said, putting his own hand over hers.

"I've got to take a shower," she said, slipping from his touch and reaching out to hook a strand of his long hair over his ear. He liked the intimate familiarity of the gesture. "I've got to get to school by seven-thirty. Playground duty."

"I'll bring you a cup of coffee when it's done."

"That would be nice," she said, and left.

Alisha taught third grade and coached in the high school. She had a master's degree in electrical engineering and a minor in American history and had married a white golf pro she met in college.

After working in Denver for six years and watching her marriage fade away as the golf pro toured and strayed, she divorced him and returned to the reservation to teach, saying she felt an obligation to give something back. Nate met her while he was scouting for a lek of sage chickens for his birds to hunt. When he first saw her she was on a long walk by herself through the knee-high sagebrush in the breaklands. She walked with purpose, talking to herself and gesticulating in the air with her hands. She had no idea he was there. When he drove up she looked directly at him with surprise. Realizing how far she had come from the res, she asked him for a ride back to her house. He invited her to climb into his Jeep, and while he drove her home, she told him she liked the idea of being back but was having trouble with reentry.

"How can you find balance in a place where the same boys who participate in a sun dance in which they seek a vision and pierce themselves are also obsessed with Grand Theft Auto and Call of Duty: Black Ops?" she asked. Nate had no answer to that.

She said her struggle was made worse when her brother Bob intimated that he always knew she would come back, since everybody did when they found out they couldn't hack it on the outside. She told Nate that during the walk she had been arguing with herself about returning, weighing the frustration of day-to-day life on the reservation and dealing with Bobby against her desire to teach the children of her friends, relatives, and tribal members. Later, Nate showed her his birds and invited her on a hunt. She went along and said she appreciated the combination of grace and savagery of falconry, and saw the same elements in him. He took it as a compliment. They went back to her house that night. That was three months ago. Now he spent at least two nights a week there.

Nate was tying his hair back into a ponytail with a rubber band when Bad Bob Whiteplume entered the kitchen from outside without knocking. Bad Bob was halfway across the kitchen before he saw Nate in the doorway.

"I smelled coffee," Bad Bob said, squinting at Nate and looking him up and down. "You're here again, huh?"

"Yes."

"Boinking my sister?"

"Say that again and we'll have to fight."

Bad Bob was shaped like a barrel and had a face as round as a hubcap. His hair was black and it glistened from the gel he used to slick the sides down and spike the top. He was wearing buckskins with a beaded front and Nike high-tops. Bob owned Bad Bob's Native American Outlet convenience store at the junction, which sold gasoline, food, and inauthentic Indian trinkets to tourists. He also rented DVDs and computer games to boys on the reservation. The back room was where the men without jobs gathered to talk and loiter and Bob held court.

Smiling and holding his hands palms up, Bob said, "Okay, I won't say it again. But your scalp would look good hanging from my lance."

"Why are you talking like an Indian?"

"I am an Indian, Kemo Sabe."

"Nah," Nate said. "Not really."

Bob poured himself a cup of coffee and sipped it, looking over the rim at Nate. "You haven't commented on my garb."

"I was waiting for you to bring it up."

"Ten of us are in a television commercial," Bob said. "They're shooting it up on the rim. The new Jeep Cherokee, I think."

Nate took a moment to say, "I guess they don't build a Northern Arapaho."

"No," Bob said, grinning, thrusting out his jaw. He was missing every other bottom tooth, so his smile reminded Nate of a jack-o'-lantern. "I'll suggest that to them, though. You should see the director. He's from L.A. He's scared of us."

"Must be the Nikes."

Bob laughed, the sound filling the room. "We told him we wouldn't do it unless they increased our talent fee from five hundred a day to seven-fifty. We scowled. He caved."

"Congratulations."

From the bathroom, Alisha called out, "Is that Bobby?"

"Good coffee!" Bob yelled back.

"Bobby, I need my television back! You've had it for a week!"

Nate looked at Bob.

"Mine went out," Bob explained. "We needed to watch the poker tournament."

Bob drained his cup and refilled it. While doing so, he saw the digital clock on the microwave. "Shit, I need to get going. They wanted to shoot with the sun at a certain angle. The director loves dawn light."

Nate said, "Who doesn't?"

"If we miss the dawn light, we just sit around until dusk and smoke cigarettes and shoot then," Bob said. "It's a good job."

"That's what counts," Nate said.

"Hey, did you hear that plane last night?" Bob asked, backing out the door so he wouldn't spill his coffee. He was taking the mug with him.

"No."

"I heard there's a big-assed jet sitting at the airport," Bob said. "Some kind of foreign writing on the fuselage."

With that, Bob left.

To himself, Nate said, *Damn.*

Nate Romanowski lived in a small stone house on the bank of the Twelve Sleep River, in the shadows of hundred-year-old cottonwoods and a high, steep bluff across the water. As he crested the long rise from the east, his place was laid out in front of him—house, round pen, sagging mews where he kept his birds—and he could tell instinctively that someone had been there.

Pulling off the two-track, he climbed out of his Jeep and walked back over to the road. Three sets of fresh tire imprints cut the night crust of the dirt where a vehicle had gone in and out and back again to his home. The tracks were wide—an SUV or a pickup. The tread was sharp, indicating new tires or a brand-new vehicle. Then he saw what had triggered his suspicion in the first place: the mews door was slightly open. Meaning his falcons had been disturbed or were gone. Which meant somebody was going to get hurt.

He stood and squinted, determining whoever had come onto his place had parked their vehicle on the side away from his house so it couldn't be seen from the road. And that they were waiting for him.

Slipping his .454 Casull handgun from its holster under his seat onto his lap, Nate drove down the rise. As he approached his house, the front door opened and a man walked out. Nate recognized the man as Ben "Shorty" LaDuke, a sometime ranch hand who resided mainly on stool number four at the Stockman's Bar in Saddlestring. Shorty had been to his house before when he was briefly employed by Bud Longbrake. Looking for strays, Shorty had said.

Shorty was diminutive with a hunched, gnome-like posture that made him look even smaller. He wore torn Wranglers and boots and a hooded Wyoming Cowboys sweatshirt.

Nate parked under the cottonwoods with his open driver's-side window framing Shorty, who ambled over. The .454 was gripped in Nate's hand, the muzzle an inch below the window.

"Nate, how are you?" Shorty asked.

"Not pleased that you're trespassing," Nate said.

"I'm sorry, but I wasn't sure where to find you. There's a feller inside who—"

"Raise your hands and turn around. Put your hands on top of your head."

Shorty grimaced. "Ah, Nate, buddy, I don't mean no trouble here."

"Then don't walk into a man's house or fuck with a falconer's birds. Do what I said."

Shorty sighed theatrically, turned, and laced his hands on top of his King Ropes cap.

Nate got slowly out of the Jeep, reached around Shorty, and patted him down. No weapons. He shoved the barrel of the .454 into Shorty's back to urge him toward the house.

"I had nothing to do with taking your birds," Shorty said. "The gentlemen inside said you owed them and they were just retrieving their property. I just said I'd make the introductions, is all."

"Don't talk," Nate said, pushing the gun into Shorty's spine.

"Be careful that don't go off," Shorty said. "It'd likely cut me in half."

Nate said, "Then you'd be really short."

He pushed him through the door, keeping the ranch hand in front of him. Over Shorty's shoulder, Nate saw two men sitting at his table with cups of coffee in front of them. They were Saudis.

"Greetings from my father," the younger of the two men said. He was olive-skinned, well-groomed, and well-dressed in a crisp white shirt, charcoal slacks, and tasseled black loafers. He had a thin, perfect mustache over perfect white teeth. The lens of a pair of wire-framed sunglasses poked up from his shirt pocket.

The other man was older, thicker, darker, wearing an open-collared yellow shirt and a black blazer. He didn't smile. His eyes were locked onto Nate's face. He had a thicker black mustache and his hands were under the table. Nate turned Shorty slightly so the older man would have to shoot through Shorty to get to Nate.

The younger man noticed what Nate had done and shook his head from side to side as if trying to alleviate a terrible misunderstanding. "No, no, none of this is necessary. Please put the gun away and let Mr. Shorty go home. We can all be good friends here."

Nate didn't move.

"I'm Lamya Abd al Saud," the man said. "Everybody I graduated with at Stanford calls me Rocky. You know my father. He says you're a talented, amazing man, but he's disappointed in you. He asked me to come here to invite you to see him to explain your recent insult."

"You know them?" Shorty said to Nate. "Jesus."

Nate ignored Shorty, keeping his eyes on the older man, watching the man's shoulders for even the smallest bit of motion from his hands hidden under the table.

"This is Khalid," Rocky said, gesturing to the dark man. "He's with me because my father asked that he come along. Khalid, please greet Mr. Romanowski."

Khalid nodded his head, but never broke his stare.

"Let me see your hands," Nate said to him.

Khalid shot a glance to Rocky. Rocky nodded back. The older man withdrew his hands from beneath the table and put them flat on the surface.

"There," Rocky said. "Are you happy now?"

"Nope. Where are my birds?"

"They're safe. My father is admiring them."

Nate said, "Admiring them?"

Rocky nodded.

"Shorty, hit the trail," Nate said, pushing the man aside.

"I don't have a vehicle," Shorty protested. "I came out here with Rocky and—"

"Hit the trail, Shorty," Nate said. "And as you walk away from this place, forget you were ever here. If anybody ever asks you to bring them out here again, your answer will be that you don't know where it is."

"They said—"

"Hit the fucking trail, Shorty," Nate said through clenched teeth.

Khalid drove and Rocky was in the passenger seat of the rented white Cadillac Escalade. Nate sat in the backseat. Khalid had asked Nate to leave the .454 at home before he would drive them.

"I've never seen a handgun like that," Rocky said. "Five cylinders. I wish to fire it."

"Wish denied," Nate said.

Khalid shot a glance at Nate in the rearview mirror.

"My father is looking forward to seeing you," Rocky said affably, turning in his seat.

Nate nodded. "Did he come here in his 727?"

Rocky shook his head. "That was his old plane. The new one is a 737. It is very luxurious, very well appointed. He prefers staying on the plane because it's more comfortable than the hotel accommodations you have here. You'll like it."

"I just want my birds back."

Rocky laughed. "I'll never understand the fascination you and my father have with falcons.

It's a mystery to me. I prefer fast cars and fast women. Blond women with big lips. And movies. I'm a great fan of American movies. Especially the gangster movies and the Westerns. I love the Westerns. I don't see why your people don't make them anymore."

Nate didn't care what Rocky liked.

Rocky gestured out the window at the sagebrush plains, the foothills, the slumping shoulders of the Bighorn Mountains. "This looks like a place for a Western movie. I expect to see a cowboy ride up any minute."

As they passed Shorty walking on the road, Nate looked out the back window. Shorty was chasing the car, his arms outstretched. Thinking that somehow they hadn't seen him.

Rocky said, "Poor Shorty."

Nate wondered if his birds were worth this.

The outsized private jet sat brilliant white and gleaming in the morning sun on the concrete apron of the Saddlestring Regional Airport. Two-foot-high Arabic writing was scrawled the length of the fuselage along with green Saudi Arabian flags. Small private planes had been moved to accommodate the craft and were parked under the wings of the 737, looking like small white offspring.

Khalid had a key to the lock on the gate and he drove the Escalade to the base of the aircraft.

"Please," Rocky said, gesturing to Nate to get out and ascend the stairs into the jet.

Al-Nura Abd al Saud, Rocky's father, sat in an overstuffed leather armchair in a book-lined private office paneled with dark rich woods and gold fixtures. A monitor and DVD player was mounted into the wall next to stacks of movies. Nate glanced at the titles, noted pornography and dozens of old Westerns: *Fort Apache*, *Red River*, *Shane*, *She Wore a Yellow Ribbon*, *The Searchers*. Al-Nura was grossly fat and soft. His robes were cream-colored cotton and they shimmered and draped when he stood up. He wore the distinctive red-and-white-checked kaffiyeh head covering held in place with a common agal band, as befit a descendant of the Royal House of Saud. Al-Nura beamed and struggled to his feet when Nate was shown into the room by Rocky.

Al-Nura took both of Nate's hands in his and shook and caressed them, saying, "It is so good to see you again, Mr. Romanowski. I was afraid something had happened to you. Please, let's sit and talk. It's time to catch up."

Rocky stood to the side, his false grin pasted on. Khalid slipped in through the doorway and closed the door behind him, taking the corner of the room where he could watch Nate and Al-Nura without moving his head.

Nate sat on a plush ottoman across from Al-Nura. The fat man settled back into his chair before the cushions had fully recovered in his absence.

"Would you like a coffee?" Al-Nura asked. "A brandy? A water? We have the whiskey you like."

"I'm fine."

Al-Nura shot a glance at Khalid. "Coffee."

Khalid crossed the room, opened another door, ordered. In a moment, a woman appeared with a silver tray with a samovar and two tiny cups. She was slim, blond, stunningly beautiful, with a full red mouth and a short black dress. She looked made-to-order for Rocky. Nate glanced over, saw the predatory look on Rocky's face, and guessed she served more than coffee.

"Thank you," Nate said as she poured him a cup.

"You're welcome," she said in a whisper. East European, Nate guessed by her accent.

"That will be all," Al-Nura said, not looking at her.

She swished out, leaving her scent in the cabin.

"I have five of those on board," Al-Nura said.

" 'Those' being women," Nate said.

Al-Nura raised his eyebrows, assessing Nate. "Yes," he said, after a beat. "All blondes. Bosnians, Albanians. They have nice women there who need jobs. There is no struggle with them. They know why they're here."

Nate shook his head, said, "We can get right to it."

Al-Nura looked at Rocky and Khalid, said,

105

"See what I told you about him? He is like this."

"No respect," Rocky said, nodding. Khalid didn't respond, but stood there dark and smoldering, his black eyes never leaving Nate.

Al-Nura laughed, a sound from deep in his chest. "All business, no sense of fun. That is Nate Romanowski, the Master Falconer."

"You have my birds," Nate said.

"Yes. But only for a while."

"I want them back."

"I can see why," Al-Nura said. "I was admiring them. Especially the peregrine. She is a cold-blooded little bitch, isn't she? I see why you prize her. If she were a woman, I would take her to my bed."

Rocky laughed at that.

Nate said, "If she were a woman, she'd turn you into a eunuch."

Rocky's laugh ended abruptly and he stepped forward. Only when Al-Nura smiled did Rocky uncoil.

"You are right," Al-Nura said. "What do you call her?"

"I call her a peregrine falcon."

"What? You don't give her a name?"

"No."

Al-Nura shook his head. "That is interesting. I've never known a falconer not to name his birds."

"I don't own them," Nate said. "We have a common interest. So I don't name them. They name themselves."

Al-Nura studied Nate, looking for something. His black eyes scoured Nate's face, his neck, his hands.

"I want a bird like that," Al-Nura said.

"I know."

"I sent you sixty thousand dollars for six young wild peregrine falcons, and the money came back without a note."

Nate nodded.

"That's not the way we do business."

"It is now."

Al-Nura sat back, his brow furrowed. "It was not enough? You've raised your prices?"

Nate reached out for the tiny cup of coffee. As he did so, he noted how Khalid tensed up and leaned forward on the balls of his feet, ready to lunge forward if necessary. Nate sipped the bitter coffee.

"Peregrines aren't rare anymore," Nate said. "They're off the endangered list. You can get them through captive breeders. You don't need to get them through me."

Al-Nura dismissed that with a quick wave of his hand. "No. I want wild birds. No captives."

"They're good birds from those programs," Nate said. "There's nothing wrong with them."

"No!" Al-Nura barked, his face flushing red.

"Wild birds only. Like yours. I am a master, I won't own domestic-raised birds."

Al-Nura started to stand but decided it wasn't worth the effort. He waved his arms as he spoke. "My people have hunted with falcons for thousands of years, it is the sport of kings. It is our tradition, my birthright. We were falconers before you even had a country. I have hunted with golden eagles from Afghanistan. I've killed deer with them. I can no longer get the eagles because of your war there. So I want the deadliest of falcons, the Rocky Mountain peregrine. The king of falcons for the sport of kings. You must help me."

Nate said nothing.

"I know that you can capture some young ones," Al-Nura said, his voice lowering from his outburst. "You know of nests here. You know where to find some."

Nate sipped the coffee.

"Here," Al-Nura said, reaching into his robes and pulling out a brick of cash. "One hundred and twenty thousand dollars. Twice what the birds should cost. I give you half of it now, the other half when you bring me the birds. And you get your falcons back. It's a good deal. You can have the Bosnian for your pleasure as well."

"I've got a woman," he said, wishing immediately he hadn't revealed that.

"I didn't fly all the way here for nothing."

Nate said, "I'm afraid you did."

His words hung there in silence. Al-Nura didn't erupt, but sat still as if he hadn't heard them. Khalid's only reaction was to shift his eyes from Nate to Al-Nura, waiting for a signal. Rocky was stunned.

"No one denies my father," Rocky whispered. "What's wrong with you?"

Nate stood up slowly so that Khalid would have no reason to react.

"Thank you for the coffee," Nate said. "I want my birds back now."

"I don't understand," Al-Nura said softly. "We've done business before. We were friends, professionals. We belong to a very small group of master falconers."

"I'm beyond that," Nate said.

"Why won't you assist me?"

Nate considered the question for a moment, said, "Because I don't like you anymore."

Al-Nura said, "Khalid."

His movement was lightning swift, too fast for Nate to ward off. Khalid was suddenly behind him, a hand on the top of his head jerking his face skyward, the bite of a razor-sharp blade like a wasp sting a quarter of an inch above his Adam's apple. Khalid pressed in with the knife. It was so sharp Nate couldn't feel the cut itself, only the thin hot stream of blood that crawled down his neck into his collar.

"Give him half of this," Al-Nura said, breaking the brick of cash and handing $60,000 to Rocky, who stuffed it into Nate's pants beneath his belt.

"You get the other half when you bring me the wild peregrines."

The next morning, an hour after dawn, Nate launched himself down the cliff face. The northern wind had picked up and was starting to buffet the tops of the cottonwood trees two hundred feet below on the banks of the stream, making a liquid sound. He was protected from the wind by the rock wall, but he could hear it howling above him as well.

He rappelled down, feeding rope through the carabiners of his harness, bouncing away from the sheer rock with the balls of his feet. Tightly coiled netting hung from his belt.

Fifty feet down was the nest. It was a huge cross-hatching of branches and twigs and dried brush, cemented together by mud, sun, and years. It was well hidden and virtually inaccessible from below, but he'd located it the year before by the whitewash of excrement that extended down the granite from the nest, looking like the results of an overturned paint bucket.

As he approached it from above, he noted the layers of building material, from the white and brittle branches on the bottom to the still-green fronds on the top. The nest had been built over generations, and had hosted falcons for forty years. Nate couldn't determine if all the inhabitants had been peregrines, but he doubted it. The original nest, he thought, had been built by eagles.

The nest came into view and Nate prepared for anything. Once, he had surprised a female raptor in the act of tearing a rabbit apart for her fledglings and the bird launched herself into his face, shredding his cheeks with her talons. But there were no mature adults in the nest. Only four downy and awkward fledglings. When they saw him, they screeched and opened their mouths wide, expecting him to give them food.

He guessed by their size that they were two months old, and would be considered eyas, too young to fly. If taken now, they would need to be immediately hooded and hand-fed until their feathers fully developed, and kept sightless in the dark so they didn't know from whom their food came. If the birds saw their owner, the falconer would be imprinted for life as the food provider and the bird would never hunt properly or maintain its wild edge. Nate didn't like taking birds this young, not only because of the work involved, but because of the moral question. He no longer wanted to own his birds, preferring instead to partner with them.

But here they were. So where was the mom? He

almost wished she would show up and drive him away.

He spun himself around and the landscape opened up as far as he could see. The sun was emerging from a bank of clouds on the eastern horizon and lighting the trees and brush with burnt orange while darkening the S curves of the river. There were no birds in the sky.

Without extracting the net from his web belt, Nate sighed, kicked himself free of the cliff face, and descended to the creek bottom.

That night, Nate sat at the back booth of the Stockman's Bar, illuminated in shadows cast by the light over the vacant pool table. The Stockman's was a long dark wooden tube of a place decorated with ancient deer and elk heads and knotty pine. There were six men at the bar sitting on stools. Shorty sat on stool number four. Shorty refused to look at Nate, who nursed a beer and waited for his friend, Wyoming game warden Joe Pickett.

At eight, the game warden entered and squinted against the gloom. Nate nodded, and Joe walked back to join him, sliding into the seat across from Nate.

"Long day," Joe said, putting his hat crown-down on the table. Joe wore his red uniform shirt with the pronghorn antelope patch on the sleeve.

"Thanks for meeting me," Nate said, signaling the barmaid for two beers.

"I can't stay long," Joe said. "I haven't been home yet. I was in the timber all day checking elk hunters."

"Find any?"

"Plenty. But you don't care about that."

"No," Nate said.

"You said something about a permit."

Nate nodded. "I need to capture a few birds."

Joe thanked the barmaid for the beer, sipped it, and studied Nate's face. "When did you decide to follow the regulations?"

"I always have."

"Like hell, Nate."

They sipped their beers.

"I stopped by your place on the way here," Joe said. "I noticed your birds were gone. I thought that was unusual."

Nate nodded.

"I don't suppose they flew off?"

"Nope."

"Does this have to do with that big jet at the airport?" Joe asked.

"Possibly."

"I always wondered what you did to make money," Joe said. "Since there's never been any visible means of support."

Nate shrugged.

Joe rolled the bottle of beer between his palms,

thinking. "I don't know if I can issue a permit when I think the purpose of capturing the falcons is to sell them."

Nate said, "That's what I thought you would say."

"Who is the potential buyer?"

"His son just entered the bar," Nate said, stealing a look over the top of the booth. Rocky and Khalid were with two of the blond women. Every eye in the place was on the women, who wore black skintight bodysuits. No women in Saddlestring had ever entered the Stockman's Bar in a bodysuit.

"Might as well look," Nate said. "Everyone else is."

Joe turned and looked, maybe a few beats longer than necessary. When he faced Nate, he said, "They don't exactly go incognito, do they?"

"They don't think they need to."

"Is that your buyer?"

"His son, Rocky. And his bodyguard."

"Who are the women?"

"Rocky's toys."

Joe paused for a while before looking up at Nate and asking, "What's really going on here?"

Nate said, "I met him years ago. He was a friend of ours in Special Forces. Not because he liked us or we liked him, but we had common interests. I never talked politics with him once. Instead, we talked falconry. He's paid me before to get him birds."

Joe said, "Hmmm."

"Al-Nura is Wahhabi. He's got billions from the royal family, and he's one of the biggest funding sources for foundations and mosques all over the world. If you're looking for one of the main guys establishing a violent religion that exists to wipe us out, you're looking at Al-Nura. Yet here he is, flying all around our country, doing as he pleases. No one even challenges him."

Nate sighed. "A guy like that can have anything in the world. If he wants peregrines, he can get them from any number of good breeding programs. Hell, he could buy the breeding program."

He jabbed a finger at Joe and lowered his voice. "But what's important to Al-Nura isn't just that he gets the falcons but that he gets them from me. It's important to him to know I can be bought. He needs to know that like all the other westerners he's ever dealt with, I have my price. It confirms his worldview."

Two more beers arrived at the booth. When Nate looked up, the barmaid said, "The man with the dollies bought the house a round."

"I don't want it," Nate said, pushing the bottle away.

"*You* tell him," the barmaid said, going back to the front.

"You're in a situation, aren't you?" Joe asked.

"Yes."

"You really don't care about a permit, do you?"

"Not really. And it gets worse," Nate said. "Alisha told me she noticed a white new-model SUV following her to school this morning. Khalid drives a rented Escalade. The description of the driver matched up. The car drove on when she pulled into the school parking lot, but they're letting me know they're ramping up the pressure."

The barmaid came back. "The gentleman who bought you the beer said to tell you he doesn't appreciate the insult."

"Tell him I still don't care what he thinks and I never will."

"Nate . . ." Joe cautioned.

"You're right," Nate said, standing. "I'll tell him myself."

"That's not what I meant," Joe said from the booth.

As Nate walked to the bar, he saw Shorty stand up and approach Rocky. Shorty was drunk.

"I don't appreciate being left out there to walk to town," Shorty said, his face red, his finger wagging in Rocky's face. "I don't care who in the hell you think you are. Out here, you don't treat a man like that, especially when he helped you out."

Rocky leaned back so Shorty's finger wouldn't touch his face. As he did so, Khalid reached through the air, grabbed Shorty's finger in his fist, and snapped it back with a sound like a dry branch breaking underfoot.

Shorty gasped, then howled. Khalid kept a grip on the finger and pulled it, and Shorty, toward the door. With his free hand, Khalid opened the door and pulled Shorty through. It happened very quickly, and no one at the bar moved or said a word.

Nate nodded at Rocky as he walked by and followed Shorty and Khalid outside. Khalid had Shorty bent over the hood of a car, facedown, while he rifled through his pockets and pulled them inside out. A wallet, loose change, and a pocketknife clattered to the pavement.

"A knife," Khalid said.

Shorty moaned, "It's just . . ."

Khalid stepped back and crouched. Nate could see what would happen next. Khalid intended to leap into the air and come down with his elbow extended to break Shorty's spine.

"You do it and it's murder," Nate said.

Khalid paused, looked over, his eyes black and glistening.

"He has a knife," Khalid said.

"Everybody carries a pocketknife," Nate said. "He never pulled it out of his pocket. You did."

"This is justifiable."

"No," Nate said, "it isn't."

A hint of a smile ghosted across Khalid's face. Nate heard the door behind him open and smelled

Rocky's cologne. Rocky must have signaled Khalid, who lunged forward with all of his weight to drive Shorty's face into the hood of the car with enough power to dent the sheet metal. Shorty crumpled back into a bloody pile, pink bubbles indicating where his nose and mouth were.

"You all saw that," Rocky said to the blondes and Khalid. "The little man had a knife."

The bartender and Joe Pickett came out of the bar and stared at Shorty. Joe ran up to make sure he was breathing.

"Call an ambulance," Joe said to the bartender.

Nate saw the smile return on Khalid. That did it. His .454 was under the driver's seat of his Jeep half a block away, but Nate wanted to take on Khalid with his hands and stepped toward him. Khalid set his feet, getting ready.

"That'll be enough of that," Sheriff McLanahan shouted.

Nate looked up to see McLanahan sticking his face through the window of a sedan that had stopped on the street.

"Mr. Romanowski, I'd suggest you call it a night and go home."

Nate squinted at the sheriff in confusion. The man wasn't in his county pickup, and wasn't in uniform. His wife sat next to him, staring straight ahead through the windshield as if she hadn't seen or heard what just transpired.

"Yes, go home," Khalid said in heavily accented English.

Joe Pickett stood up. "Sheriff, we have an injured man here."

"I heard it on the scanner," McLanahan said. "The ambulance is on its way. And stay out of this, Joe."

"I saw what happened. Nate wasn't at fault."

"He never is," McLanahan said, moving his eyes from Joe to Nate. "It just seems like wherever he shows up, people get hurt or killed."

"Go home," Khalid taunted, now smiling widely.

Nate looked over McLanahan's new car. It had dealer plates and the sticker was still in the window.

"Nice ride," Nate said. "I hope it was worth it."

McLanahan's wife continued to stare stonily ahead, but Nate thought he saw her wince a little. McLanahan's face got red, which looked dark in the glow of the streetlight.

"This is what they do," Nate said. "They buy us with our own money. Your price was pretty damned cheap."

"Move on," McLanahan said through gritted teeth.

Nate felt a tug on his arm. Joe. "The odds aren't good right now," he whispered. Nate loved Joe at that moment. Joe wasn't telling him to back off, or give up, or go home. Instead, he was advising Nate to regroup and fight later, when he held the high ground. The thought calmed him.

Rocky walked between Nate and Khalid. "No more trouble," Rocky said. "Let's all go back in and enjoy another drink. I'm buying, my friends. This is over."

Nate said, "I don't think so."

Nate walked away and Joe stayed with Shorty. As Nate climbed into his Jeep, he looked down the street toward the Stockman's. Rocky was patting backs and shaking hands, offering loudly to buy the house another round, not even looking over his shoulder as the ambulance appeared from around the block. McLanahan had parked his new car and was joining them.

"He's out there," Alisha said. "I can feel it."

Nate threw off the quilts and his bare feet slapped the floor of her bedroom. A trough of moonlight split the floor. He approached the window, but didn't open the curtains farther.

Nate said, "I can see the grille of the car shining in the moon. It's parked behind the willows out front."

She said, "Are you sure it's him?"

"Who else would drive a white Cadillac onto the res?" he said.

She reached for the bed lamp but Nate stopped her, whispered, "Keep it dark in here."

• • •

Nate smelled the smoke of strong cigarettes long before he saw the car. He had gone out the back door of Alisha's house, forded the creek, and looped far around her lot so he could approach the Escalade from behind. He kept inside the brush, breathing evenly, stepping slowly and quietly, his gun hanging loosely at his side.

The interior of the SUV was dark, but as Nate stood and looked, letting his eyes adjust, he could see the familiar blocky head at three-quarter-rear profile behind the wheel. Khalid turned his head slightly and Nate could see the orange glow of his cigarette ash.

Nate looked around. The powwow grounds near Alisha's home were empty except for the naked pole frames of tipis and the tall sun dance pole that shone blue in the moonlight. Dried leather ropes hung down from the sun dance pole and waved gently like kelp in the night breeze. The structures should have been dismantled weeks ago, after the powwow, but in the Indian way, they weren't.

Nate thought of his birds. He thought of Shorty's face bubbling blood. He thought of that white Escalade following Alisha to school. And he thought of mosques and madrassas all over the world teaching the young to hate.

Khalid was genuinely surprised when Nate reached in through his window and snatched the cigarette out of his mouth, and he started to say something but his open mouth filled with the huge muzzle of a .454.

"Do you know what a sun dance is?" Nate asked. "It's a way for a boy to become a man."

The curtain parted on a cabin window of the 737 and Rocky looked out. Even at that height and distance, Rocky's face looked pale and his eyes bleary from alcohol and lack of sleep. It was minutes before dawn and the western sky was washed with a deep pink about to dissolve into the first blast of morning sun.

Nate stood up in his Jeep and gestured to the heavy wooden crate that filled his backseat. There were holes in the crate.

Rocky's face vanished from the window.

Nate stood in the cold of dawn, feeling the last rush of icy pre-morning breeze flow across the tarmac as if looking for a place to hide until it was dark again. A meadowlark warbled somewhere behind him.

Nate turned to the crate. He could hear the rustle of feathers, and one of the birds answered the meadowlark with a sharp chirp.

The door of the airplane opened. Rocky stood in a bathrobe, one hand shielding his eyes from the light and the other waving Nate in. Nate climbed the stairs carrying the crate, and he could smell fetid alcohol and strong garlicky sweat through Rocky's skin. "Late night, huh?"

"Come in, come in, so I can close the door."

Nate stepped inside the dark cabin.

"You brought the birds?" Rocky asked.

"What does it look like?" Nate asked.

Rocky nodded, uncomprehending. "You are here much too early. Let me wake my father."

Nate sat while Rocky walked gingerly through the cabin, as if the sound of his footsteps hurt his head. The darkness of the plane seemed to have calmed the birds in the crate, although he could still hear them rustling inside. In a few minutes, Nate heard the low rumble of Arabic through the door.

While he waited, Nate perused the movie library and selected *Fort Apache* with John Wayne. John Ford directing. A classic. He got it running and the dark cabin flickered with screaming Indians and frightened soldiers.

Al-Nura entered fitting his headscarf on. Nate appreciated the formality, in a way.

"You are early," Al-Nura said, settling down in his big chair. Rocky followed. Al-Nura's eyes lit up when he noticed the crate. "Six of them?"

"Seven, actually," Nate said.

"You flatter me."

Nate said nothing. He listened for the sound of a vehicle outside on the tarmac.

Rocky lit a cigarette with trembling fingers. "We kept the bar open until very early this morning," he said. "The owner wanted to close at two, but we sweetened the pot for him. The whole town had a wonderful time."

"It wasn't the whole town," Nate said. "Just some drunks and derelicts. Your friend Khalid wasn't with you, though."

Rocky looked up, the match still burning in his fingers. His ever-present smile was missing.

Nate said, "He was with me."

Al-Nura used his hands on the arms of the chair to turn himself so he could see Rocky behind him. Father and son exchanged glances.

"Where is he now?" Rocky asked, almost in a whisper.

"Outside."

"Let me see the birds," Al-Nura said, turning back to Nate. His eyes were hard.

"Where are my falcons?" Nate asked.

Al-Nura gestured outside with his chin. "They are safe in the hangar we rented. It's the second one from the left out there. They've been watered and well fed."

Nate nodded, backed up, and pried the lid off the crate. The birds began to chirp furiously when exposed to light.

Al-Nura asked quickly, "Are they hooded?"

"Nope."

"They'll see us!" he said angrily. "They'll be imprinted for life!"

"You said—"

"Close the box!"

Nate put the lid back on. While he fastened the clips, a horn honked outside. Rocky looked at the curtained window, then back to Nate.

"You asked about Khalid," Nate said, gesturing toward the window.

Rocky inhaled deeply on the cigarette and crossed the cabin to the window and brushed the curtain aside. Nate watched Rocky's eyes widen and the cigarette dropped from his fingers, then Rocky stumbled backward, flailing his arms.

"What?" Al-Nura asked his son. "What has happened?"

"Khalid . . ." was all Rocky could say.

The sound of war cries erupted from the monitor as the Apaches attacked the fort.

Al-Nura reached up and opened the curtain. Nate could tell from Al-Nura's lack of alarm that he had seen worse in his life, and it had probably been on his orders. *Bastard,* Nate thought.

It had taken two hours to mount the sun dance pole onto the back of the flatbed truck, spearing it through a missing fifth-wheel mount on the truck bed. But it had taken only twenty minutes to hang Khalid from the leather ropes from sharpened bones pierced deeply through his pectorals. Now the bodyguard was suspended in the air, his hands limp at his sides, his face tilted to the sky.

"He comes to every once in a while," Nate said. "He screams a bunch of crap in Arabic, then he passes out again."

"How could you do that to a man?" Rocky said, his face contorted.

"It's not so bad," Nate said. "I did it once myself. But when he gets cut down, he'll be a warrior."

Al-Nura swiveled slowly to Nate, his face a mask. But Nate could see his lower lip tremble involuntarily.

"It's time for you to go," Nate said. "You've got five minutes to order your pilot to fire up the jets."

Al-Nura was frozen with rage. He looked like he wanted to leap out of the chair and attack Nate with his hands.

"You don't threaten my father," Rocky said.

Nate nodded toward the windows on the other side of the plane. "Check that out," he said.

Nate didn't even need to look because he knew what Rocky would see: a dozen Northern Arapaho warriors in full dress on horseback on the edge of the tarmac, feathers from lances and rifles riffling in the breeze.

"Just like *Fort Apache*," Nate said.

Al-Nura slowly shook his head back and forth. "You'll never get the rest of the money," he said.

"Don't need it," Nate said. "And don't ever

contact me again or you and your little boy will end up on the sun dance pole, too."

"But don't you want the money?" Al-Nura asked.

"I'll be the first: no."

With that, Nate opened the hatch and clambered down the steps. He helped Bad Bobby Whiteplume cut Khalid down. The man stumbled toward the plane as the jet engines started up. Nate watched Khalid climb up the stairs on his hands and knees and wondered for a moment if Rocky would shut the door on him before he got in. Khalid made it, barely, without ever looking back. Twin spoors of blood snaked up the aluminum steps from Khalid's wounds.

The door closed behind him and the stairs scissored back into place and Nate and Bob drove their vehicles to the side of the airport, where they met the warriors. The roar of the plane shook the ground itself and split the sky in two.

While the 737 rose into the air, Nate checked the birds in the hangar. The peregrine screamed at him when he opened the door. He rejoined Bob and Bob's crew with the hooded falcon on his fist.

It was minutes before the jet was far enough away that they could hear themselves speak.

Bad Bob yawned. "Too damned early for this kind of stuff."

Several men agreed. They had all dismounted and held their horses by the reins.

"Any of you ever see *Fort Apache*?" Nate asked.

"You mean *Fort Apache, the Bronx*?" one of them asked. "With Paul Newman and Ed Asner?"

"Pam Grier was in that, too," Bob said.

"No," Nate said. "The original. With John Wayne."

No one had.

"Here," Nate said to Bob. "Our deal."

He gave Bob half of the brick of Al-Nura's cash. Bob started to count it as the others gathered around him. Bob lost count, looked up at Nate, said, "I trust you. Besides, I know where to find you at my sister's place."

A couple of the men laughed.

"Not a bad gig," one of them said, nodding at the 737, which was a dot against the belly of a cumulus cloud.

"You can still make the shoot," Nate said, looking up. "The light is still good."

"Fuck the Cherokee thing," Bob said. "This is much better. Call on us anytime you need Indians."

"I hope I don't need you again," Nate said.

"You don't think he'll come back?"

"No. We screwed up his worldview."

Bob said, "Whatever that means."

As Nate climbed into his Jeep, Bob broke off

128

from his friends and approached him. Bob had a threatening expression on his face, the one he had no doubt used on the film location to get more money from the director.

"What?"

"I've got a question," Bob said in a gravel voice.

"Ask away."

"Does this cover the seven chickens you took from my coop?" Then Bad Bob broke into a grin.

Nate smiled back and peeled off two more bills. "This should cover the chickens," he said, "with change left over to buy some coffee and your own television set."

EVERY DAY IS
A GOOD DAY
ON THE RIVER

The guide, Randall "Call Me Duke" Conner, pushed them off from the sandy launch below the bridge into the river and within seconds the muscular dark flow of the current gripped the flat-bottomed McKenzie boat and spun it like a cigarette butt in a flushed toilet. The morning was cool but sunny and there was enough of a breeze to rattle the dry fall leaves in the cottonwoods that reached out over the water like skeletal hands. There were three men in the boat. Jack, who'd never been in a drift boat before, cried out: "Is this safe, Duke?"

"Ha!" Duke snorted. "Of course. Just let me get at the oars and get us turned around. Everything will be just fine. It's a good day on the river. Every day is a good day on the river."

Duke stepped around Jack, who had the front fishing seat in the bow. The boat bucked with his weight. Jack reached out and grasped the casting leg brace in front of his seat and held on and slightly closed his eyes until Duke got settled in the middle of the boat and it stopped rocking. The guide grasped the oars and with two quick and powerful strokes—forward on the left oar, backward on the right—stopped the boat from spinning and righted it within the flow.

Duke said, "See, we're perfectly fine now. You can relax. It's Jack, isn't it?"

"Yes, it's Jack."

Duke nodded, then spoke in a pleasant, soft voice. What he said was well rehearsed. "This is a McKenzie-style drift boat, Jack, the finest of its kind. It was designed for western rivers like this. Flat-bottomed, flared sides, a narrow pointed stern, and extreme rocker in the bow and stern to allow the boat to spin around on its center like a pivot. It's not sluggish like a raft or a damned tank like a jon boat. We point the bow toward one of the banks downriver and keep the stern upriver and we use the power of the river to move us along. That's why it's called a drift boat! I use the oars to keep us in the right place for fishing. Hell, I can shoot this boat from side to side across the river like a skeeter bug to get you fishermen in the best possible position for catching fish, Jack. That's why we float at a forty-five-degree angle to the current, so both of you will have clear fishing lanes and you won't have to cast over each other. It's stable as hell, so don't be afraid to stand up in that brace and cast. Just make sure you keep balanced, Jack. And try not to hook me in the ear on your back cast!"

Duke had a deep laugh that Jack would describe as infectious if he were in the right mood.

Jack found out his fishing seat would turn on its pedestal. He released the leg brace and cautiously spun the seat around so he could watch Duke work the oars. The guide was a magician, an expert, and he could move the boat with a flick of either oar. Duke was tall, with powerful shoulders from rowing, no doubt. He had a big sweeping mustache and a dark tan. He wore a fishing shirt, shorts, and river sandals. His eyes were hidden by dark sunglasses fitted with a strap so he could hang them from his neck. Forceps were clipped to a breast pocket as were clippers strung from a retractable zinger. He had a big wolfish smile full of perfect white teeth. Jack thought, *He's a man's man. One of those men, like skiing instructors or firemen, who just seem to have everything they ever wanted in life.*

Jack watched as Duke turned around and looked over his shoulder at the other fisherman, Jack's host, in the seat in the bow of the boat.

Duke looked over his shoulder. "And you're Tim, right?"

"Yes," Tim said wearily.

Jack turned in his chair. Tim looked small and slight and scrunched up in comparison with Duke. Jack thought Tim looked like a wet mouse, even though he was dry. Maybe it was the way Tim sat, all pulled into himself, hunched over in his seat, his chin down against his chest. He wore an oversized rain jacket, waders, and a ridiculous hat with hidden earflaps tucked up under the band. Jack shot a look toward the northern horizon to see if there were thunderheads rolling. Nope.

Duke said, "So it's Jack and Tim. You guys seem like a couple of hale fellows well met. Did you say you've fished this river before?"

Jack said he was new to drift boat fishing, but he was willing to learn the ropes. Jack confessed, "I've never fished with a guide before. This is all a new experience. But when Tim asked me to come along, I jumped all over the opportunity. So just tell me what to do, I don't mind."

"That's a good way to be, Jack. We'll have a good time. What about you, Tim?"

Tim didn't answer. He stared at the water on the side of the boat as if the foam and bubbles were the most fascinating thing he'd ever seen. The only sounds were the metal-on-metal squeak of the oars in the oarlocks and the rapid *lap-lap-lap* of the water on the side of the fiberglass hull.

Again, Duke said, "Tim, what about you?"

Finally, Tim looked up. There was something mean in his eyes and his lips were pulled against his teeth so hard they looked translucent.

"Duke, why do you say our names every time you ask a question, Duke? Is that so you'll remember our names, *Duke?* Is that one of your guide tricks, *Duke?*"

Then he added, in an icy tone Jack had never heard Tim use before: "Your name is Randall, but you go by Duke. I think I'll call you Randall, Randall."

Duke flashed an uncomfortable smile and looked up at Jack instead of over his shoulder at Tim. As if trying to get Jack to acknowledge Tim was out of line. The silence between them grew uncomfortable until Duke finally shrugged it off and filled it.

"Someone wake up on the wrong side of the bunk this morning? Well, never mind that, Tim. Everything will change, Tim. Every day is a good day on the river. We just haven't caught any fish yet because we haven't been fishing. So let's just get you fellows rigged up. I'll pull over here into this little back eddy and drop the anchor and get you rigged up. Everything will be fine once you hook up with one of these monsters."

Tim rolled his eyes and said, *"What crap. Jesus Christ."*

Jack had never heard Tim talk with such sarcasm before, and he was a little shocked. He tried to cover for his host. Jack said, "Tim's been all over the West on all the famous rivers, right, Tim? The Bighorn, the Big Hole, the Wind, the Madison, the North Fork, and of course here on the North Platte. He always tells me about his trips. So when he invited me on this one, man, I jumped at the chance."

Duke said, "So you've gotten around, eh, Tim?"

"I'm not the only one, Randall."

Jack shook his head. Tim seemed so out of character, so bitter. He thought, *Something is going on here*. He wondered if rich men treated guides this way. If so, he didn't think he liked it.

Jack heard a heavy splash and he turned around in his seat again. He'd seen the anchor hanging from an arm off the back of the boat and now it was gone. The anchor was ten scarred pounds of pyramid-shaped lead. It was triggered to drop by a foot release under Duke's rowing bench. Jack could feel the boat slow and then stop when the anchor bit into the riverbed and the boat swung around into the current.

Duke spoke to Jack as if he hadn't heard Tim's earlier statement.

"We'll get you started with nymphs and an indicator. When we get rigged up, throw it out there and keep an eye on the indicator, Jack. If you see it tick or bounce, you raise the rod tip fast. Sometimes these fish barely lip the nymph. So if you see that indicator do anything at all, set the hook."

Jack nodded. "Okay."

"It's easy to get mesmerized by the indicator in the water, so don't worry about that. We only have one place on the river where it gets a little hairy, and that's the place downriver called the Chutes. You've probably heard of it."

"I have. Didn't somebody die there last year?"

"About one a year, actually," Duke said, stripping lengths of tippet from a spool to build the nymph rig and tying knots with the deft movements of a surgeon. "There are big rocks on both sides and some rapids down the middle. But as long as you hit the middle squared up, there's no problem. I've done it a hundred times and never flipped a boat. That's the only place you'll need to reel in for a few minutes and you may get a little splash of water on you since you're in front. Otherwise, don't worry about a thing. Tim, do you want me to tie on a couple of nymphs for you?"

"I'll do it myself."

"Suit yourself, Tim."

"I will, *Randall*."

Jack really didn't know Tim well enough to claim they were friends. So he had been surprised when Tim called him at his construction company the week before and offered to host him on a guided fishing trip on the North Platte River. Jack had said yes before checking his calendar or with his wife, Janey, even with the odd provision Tim had requested.

Later, Jack had told Janey about the invitation and the terms of the provision. She was making dinner at the stove—spaghetti and meat sauce—and she shook her head and made a puzzled face.

She said, "He wants you to make the booking? I didn't think you knew him all that well."

"I don't. But yes, he asked me to use my credit card for the deposit, but said he'd pay me back for everything afterward, including the flies we use and the tip. He wanted to make sure we were scheduled to go on the river with the owner of the guide service—somebody named Duke—and no one else. He said it was important to go with the owner because we'd catch the most fish that way. Who was I to argue? Tim wants the best, I guess."

"But why you?"

Jack shrugged. "I guess he remembers I was the only one who never gave him any shit in high school when we were growing up. Everybody else did because he was such a weird dude. And he was. You've seen that picture of him in the yearbook. But hell, I guess I always sort of felt sorry for him. For some reason, I liked him and I kind of sympathized with the little creep. His parents were real no-hopers, and for a while the whole family lived in their car. That car was just filled with junk—sleeping bags and crap. They'd drop him off for school on the street we lived on so nobody would know, but I saw him get out once. He was real embarrassed, but I didn't tell anyone I saw him. I guess he appreciated that. He told me once he never wanted to live in a car again. A high school kid telling me that, I don't know. I was sort of touched. Man, I sound lame."

She laughed and said, "You do, honey, but that will be our little secret. Then he invented that thing—what was it?"

"You're asking me? Hell, I'm not sure. Somebody explained it to me once but it didn't take. Something about a circuit for a wireless router or something. Whatever it was, it made him millions."

She pursed her lips and said, "And he moved back home to Wyoming. I always thought that was strange."

"Yeah, me too. He coulda lived anywhere."

"Jack," she asked, while making a sly face at him, "if you made tens of millions, would you move?"

Jack snorted and rolled his eyes. "We won't have to worry about finding out. I'll never have to make that decision, so you better keep your job."

"Bummer," she said, and changed the subject. "And he got married to that bombshell. What is her name?"

He could see her in his mind's eye: tall, black hair, green eyes, great figure. A bit much, but that was the point, he thought. But her name? "I can't remember," he said.

She said, "I saw them together once. Beauty and the Geek, that's for sure."

"Maybe he wanted to prove something to all the jocks and high school big shots who used to pants him and hang him upside down from a tree, like, *Look at me, losers!*"

"But he asked *you* to go fishing with him."

"Yeah, and I want to go."

"Maybe he thinks you're his best friend. That's kind of sweet and pathetic at the same time."

"Oh, bullshit," Jack said, looking away. "I just want to catch big trout with a five-hundred-dollar-a-day guide. That's the big time, baby. Every man wants to fish with flies and catch a big trout. Here's my chance."

Jack caught two large trout before noon with the nymphs and missed at least five more. The fish he boated and Duke netted were a rainbow and a brown. The trout were big, thick, and sleek and reminded him of wet quadriceps muscles that happened to have a head, fins, and a tail. Both were over twenty-two inches. When the fish took the nymphs, it was as if an electric current shot up through the line to his rod, as if they'd like to pull him out of the boat and into the water. He'd whooped and Duke dropped the anchor with a splash and reached for his big net. Jack couldn't remember when he had had so much fun.

Tim caught ten, but netted them himself without a word, and Duke simply shrugged and said, "Let me know if you need any help."

"I don't. I do things for myself."

The rhythm of the current lulled Jack. He stared at the indicator until the image of it burned into his mind, and its bobbing mesmerized him. At one point he looked up and thought the boat and indicator were stationary in the river, but the banks were rolling by, and not the other way around. There were bald eagles in some of the trees—Duke pointed them out in a way that suggested he did the same thing every day—and they floated by mule deer drinking in the water and a family of river otters slip-sliding over one another on some rocks.

Duke kept up a steady patter.

"River right there's a nice hole."

"Nice cast there, Jack."

"Don't forget to mend your line. There, that's the ticket."

"If you hook up again, use your reel. That's what it's there for. Don't grab the line. Don't horse it in."

"What a beautiful day. Every day is a good day on the river, ain't it?"

All of the land they were floating through was private, with just a few public spots marked by blue diamond-shaped signs mounted on T-posts. There were few houses or buildings along the shores and it seemed to Jack they were the only people on the river or, perhaps, on the planet. There were no take-out spots anywhere, and the truck and trailer would be miles ahead by now, he guessed.

He thought: *Once you're on the river, you're on the river for the rest of the day. You can't stop and go home. You can't get out. There's nowhere to go.*

• • •

Although he was concentrating on the gentle bobbing of the strike indicator, Jack saw—or thought he saw—an odd movement in his peripheral vision from the back of the boat. When he turned his head and looked directly, he saw Tim pulling his arm back and jamming his hand into the pocket of his coat. There had been something black in his hand and his arm had been outstretched, but whatever it was was now hidden, and Tim wouldn't look up and meet his eyes. Instead, Tim made a beautiful cast toward the opposite bank.

Jack shook his head and rotated back around in his chair. What had been in Tim's hand? And why did he think it might have been a gun pointed at the back of Duke's head?

Then Jack thought: *Stop being ridiculous.*

Duke backed the boat to the bank and dropped the anchor on the dirt with a heavy thud and said, "How about some lunch, guys?"

Jack had already reeled in because he could hear the increasing roar downriver. The sound was heavy and angry. He asked, "Is that the Chutes up ahead, Duke?"

"That's it, all right. But we'll grab some lunch here first."

Jack was hungry and it felt good to step on hard ground and stretch his legs and back. Duke had said the camp was leased from a rancher exclusively for Duke and his fishing guides and it had a picnic table, a fire pit, and an outhouse. Tim headed for the outhouse first, and Jack followed. Duke stayed back at the camp and started a fire in the pit and dug items out of his cooler.

When Tim finally stepped from the outhouse, Jack smiled at him. "I really want to thank you again for inviting me along. This is really special."

"Sure, Jack," Tim said. But he seemed distracted.

Jack hesitated, wondering how to put it. Then he said, "Is everything okay, Tim? I know we don't know each other all that well, but, well . . . Are you feeling okay?"

Tim looked up sharply. *"Why do you ask?"*

"Is there something between you and Duke, or am I just imagining things?"

Tim looked hard at Jack, as if searching his face for something or wondering what he should reply.

Jack said, "A while back, I looked in the back of the boat and I thought I saw something."

"Really?"

"Yes. But I might have been imagining things."

In response, Tim reached up and patted Jack's shoulder as he walked past him. He said, "I shouldn't have gotten you involved. I'm sorry."

"Involved in what?"

But Tim was gone, walking alone toward the river far to the right of the camp.

Jack and Duke sat at the picnic table and ate hamburgers. Jack ate two and half a tube of Pringles. He washed it all down with two cans of Coors Light. He said to Duke, "I can't believe I'm so hungry."

"Being outside does that to you."

"The burgers were great, thank you."

"You're paying for them," Duke laughed, then shouted toward Tim, who was still standing alone on the bank, watching the river flow by. "Tim, are you sure you don't want lunch? You've got to be starving, man."

Tim didn't reply. Duke leaned across the table and lowered his voice. "To each his own, I guess. Is he always this surly?"

"No."

"I never got his last name. What is it?"

"Hey, I really don't like gossiping about my host, if you don't mind."

"Sorry," Duke said, "I should mind my own business. You're right. Oh well, I've had worse in the boat. Luckily, I'm a people person. You have to be a people person to be a guide."

"I guess you get some characters, eh?"

Duke laughed and shook his head from side to side. "You have no idea, Jack. You have no idea."

Duke packed up the lunch items and secured the cooler to the floor of the boat with bungee cords.

Jack waited on the bank, looking downriver toward the roar. He said to Duke, "You say there's nothing to worry about, right?"

"Right," Duke said, chinning toward the Chutes. "I've done it a million times and haven't lost a fisherman yet. And right past the rapids is one of the deepest holes in the whole river. You'll need to be ready to cast out as soon as we clear the rapids. We'll for sure pick up some fish in there."

"Jack, I'll take the front this time."

Jack turned. He hadn't noticed that Tim had joined them. Tim's face was ashen, and he looked gaunt.

Jack asked, "Are you sure? Duke says it gets a little splashy in front."

"Yes. Please, Jack, step aside."

Tim shouldered past Jack and stepped into the front of the boat and took the seat. He swiveled it around so it was backward and he faced Duke, who was already on the oars. Duke ignored Tim and spoke to Jack.

"I'll swing the boat around so you can get in the back easy."

Tim had his hand in his parka pocket and when he withdrew it he held a snub-nosed revolver. He pointed it at Duke's face, not more than two feet away from him.

Tim said, *"Start rowing."*

Duke's face reddened. "Hey! What the fuck are you doing?"

Tim said, "I said start rowing. Pull up the anchor. We're leaving Jack here. He doesn't need to see this."

Duke spread his arms, palms out. "Jesus, this is a joke, right? It's a joke?"

Jack stood on the bank with his mouth gaped. Tim spoke to him without taking his eyes, or the muzzle of his gun, off Duke.

He said, "I'm sorry, Jack. I'm sorry I used you and brought you along. But I was afraid Randall would recognize my name if I made the booking. I'm sure Amanda told him my name."

Jack noticed that the blood had drained from Duke's face. Amanda, that was Tim's wife's name. Amanda.

Tim said, "Right, Randall? Right? She told you my name. She called you and told you when I was going on a business trip? Or a fishing trip? So you two could get together and humiliate me in my own hometown? Right in front of dozens of people who know me? I know all about it, Randall. Did you laugh at me when you were in my bed? Did you laugh because I was so stupid?"

"Look," Duke pleaded, "it was Mandy's idea. Really. We never laughed at you."

"Mandy, is it? She never asked me to call her Mandy. It's a stupid name. Like Randall. Or Duke." A few wisps of Tim's hair had dislodged from his scalp and hung down over his eye.

Duke said, "You don't have to do this. This is crazy. Look, I'll never see her again. I fucking swear it, man."

Tim's smile was terrifying. He said, "No, you'll never see her again. You're right about that. No one will ever see her again."

He let it sink in.

Duke moaned, *"Oh, God. No."*

"Yes," Tim said. "This morning. In that bed you know so well. She thought I was bending over to kiss her good-bye. And in a way, I was."

Jack didn't realize he was unconsciously stepping away from the boat until the picnic table hit him in the back of the thighs. The roaring in his ears drowned out the sound of the Chutes. Tim shouted to be heard over it.

"I'm sorry, Jack. I'm sorry to leave you here. But there's a ranch house a couple of miles away. You'll be fine."

Jack said, "Tim, don't do this. Please, Tim."

"Too late, I'm afraid. They laughed at me, Jack. That's the worst thing anyone can do to me. Remember how they used to laugh at me in school?"

"That was a long time ago, Tim. You're a big man now. You're a good man."

Tim said to Duke, "No one laughs at me."

Jack watched Tim say something else to Duke, and the boat slipped out into the current and was gone. Because of the heavy brush downriver, he lost sight of it quickly, but began to run parallel to the river, hoping he could catch them ahead on a bend. Hoping he could persuade Tim to pull the boat over before it picked up too much speed entering the Chutes and he'd lose them. And before Tim did something he'd regret.

Jack stopped when he heard the sharp crack of a shot. Then he lowered his shoulder and forced himself through the brush. Thorns tore his flesh and his clothing, and his face was bleeding when he broke through and stood knee-deep in the cold water.

The boat was a long way downriver. Beyond it Jack could see the huge boulders in the river and the foam of whitewater. Duke was bent over the oars, his head forward, his arms hanging limply at his sides. Tim had swiveled his chair around, his back to Duke's body, to face the Chutes. Tim stood up in the fishing platform and braced himself. He tossed the gun into the water and reached up and clamped his hat on tight and then raised his chin to the oncoming rapids.

Jack shouted but couldn't even hear himself. The boat began a lazy turn sidewise.

PRONGHORNS
OF THE THIRD REICH

As he did every morning, Paul Parker's deaf and blind old Labrador, Champ, signaled his need by burrowing his nose into Parker's neck and snuffling. If Parker didn't immediately throw back the covers and get up, Champ would woof until he did. So he got up. The dog used to bound downstairs in a manic rush and skid across the hardwood floor of the landing to the back door, but now he felt his way down slowly with his belly touching each stair, grunting with each step, and his big nose serving as a kind of wall bumper. Champ steered himself, Parker thought, via echo navigation. Like a bat. It was sad. Parker followed and yawned and cinched his robe tight and wondered how many more mornings there were left in his dog.

Parker glanced at his reflection in a mirror in the stairwell. Six-foot-two, steel-gray hair, cold blue eyes, and a jawline that was starting to sag into a dewlap. Parker hated the sight of the dewlap, and unconsciously raised his chin to flatten it. Something else: he looked tired. Worn and tired. He looked like someone's old man. Appearing in court used him up these days. Win or lose, the trials just took his energy out of him and it took longer and longer to recharge. As

Champ struggled ahead of him, he wondered if his dog remembered *his* youth.

He passed through the kitchen. On the counter was the bourbon bottle he had forgotten to cap the night before, and the coffeemaker he hadn't filled or set. He looked out the window over the sink. Still dark, overcast, spitting snow, a sharp wind quivering the bare branches of the trees. The cloud cover was pulled down like a window blind in front of the distant mountains.

Parker waited for Champ to get his bearings and find the back door. He took a deep breath and reached for the door handle, preparing himself for a blast of icy wind in his face.

Clint and Juan stood flattened and hunched on either side of the back door of the lawyer's house on the edge of town. They wore balaclavas and coats and gloves. Clint had his stained gray Stetson clamped on his head over the balaclava, even though Juan had told him he looked ridiculous.

They'd been there for an hour in the dark and cold and wind. They were used to conditions like this, even though Juan kept losing his focus, Clint thought. In the half-light of dawn, Clint could see Juan staring off into the backyard toward the mountains, squinting against the pinpricks of snow. As if pining for something, which was probably the warm weather of Chihuahua. Or a warm bed. More than once,

Clint had to lean across the back porch and cuff Juan on the back of his skull and tell him to get his head in the game.

"What game?" Juan said. His accent was heaviest when he was cold, for some reason, and sounded like, *Wha' gaaaame?*

Clint started to reach over and shut Juan up when a light clicked on inside the house. Clint hissed, "Here he comes. Get ready. *Focus.* Remember what we talked about."

To prove that he heard Clint, Juan scrunched his eyes together and nodded.

Clint reached behind him and grasped the Colt .45 1911 ACP with his gloved right hand. He'd already racked in a round, so there was no need to work the slide. He cocked it and held it alongside his thigh.

Across the porch, Juan drew a .357 Magnum revolver from the belly pocket of the Carhartt hoodie he wore.

The back door opened and the large blocky head of a dog poked out looking straight ahead. The dog grunted as it stepped down onto the porch and waddled straightaway, although Juan had his pistol trained on the back of its head. It was Juan's job to watch the dog and shoot it dead if necessary.

Clint reached up and grasped the outside door handle and jerked it back hard.

Paul Parker tumbled outside in a heap, robe flying, blue-white bare legs exposed. He scrambled over to his hands and knees in the snow-covered grass and said, "Jesus Christ!"

"No," Clint said, aiming the pistol at a spot on Parker's forehead. "Just us."

"What do you want?"

"What's coming to me," Clint said. "What I deserve and you took away."

A mix of recognition and horror passed over Parker's face. Clint could see the fear in the lawyer's eyes. It was a good look as far as Clint was concerned. Parker said, "Clint? Is that you?"

What could Clint want? Parker thought. There was little of significant value in the house. Not like Engler's place out in the country, that book collection of western Americana. But Clint? He *was* a warped version of western Americana. . . .

"Get up and shut the hell up," Clint said, motioning with the Colt. "Let's go in the house where it's warm."

Next to Parker, Champ squatted and his urine steamed in the grass.

"It don' even know we're here," Juan said. "Some watchdog. I ought to put it out of its misery." *Meeserie.*

"Please don't," Parker said, standing up. "He's my bird dog and he's been a great dog over the years. He doesn't even know you're here." Clint noticed Parker had dried grass stuck to his bare knees.

"You don't look like such a hotshot now without your lawyer suit," Clint said.

"I hope you got some hot coffee, mister," Juan said to Parker.

"I'll make some."

"Is your wife inside?" Clint asked.

"No."

Clint grinned beneath his mask. "She left you, huh?"

"Nothing like that," Parker lied. "She's visiting her sister in Sheridan."

"Anybody inside?"

"No."

"Don't be lying to me."

"I'm not. Look, whatever it is—"

"Shut up," Clint said, gesturing with his Colt. "Go inside slowly and try not to do something stupid."

Parker cautiously climbed the step and reached out for the door Clint held. Clint followed. The warmth of the house enveloped him, even through his coat and balaclava.

Behind them, Juan said, "What about the dog?"

"Shoot it," Clint said.

"Jesus God," Parker said, his voice tripping.

A few seconds later there was a heavy boom and simultaneous yelp from the backyard, and Juan came in.

Paul Parker sat in the passenger seat of the pickup and Clint sat just behind him in the crew cab with the muzzle of his Colt kissing the nape of his neck. Juan drove. They left the highway and took a two-track across the sagebrush foothills eighteen miles from town. They were shadowed by a herd of thirty to forty pronghorn antelope. It was late October, almost November, and the grass was brown and snow from the night before pooled in the squat shadows of the sagebrush. The landscape was harsh and bleak and the antelope had been designed perfectly for it: their brown-and-white coloring melded with the terrain and at times it was as if they were absorbed within it. And if the herd didn't feel comfortable about something—like the intrusion of a beat-up 1995 Ford pickup pulling an empty rattletrap stock trailer behind it—they simply flowed away over the hills like molten lava.

"Here they come again," Juan said to Clint. It was his truck and they'd borrowed the stock trailer from an outfitter who got a new one. "They got so many antelopes out here."

"Focus," Clint said. He'd long since taken off the mask—no need for it now—and stuffed it in his coat pocket.

Parker stared straight ahead. They'd let him put on pajamas and slippers and a heavy lined winter topcoat and that was all. Clint had ordered him to bring his keys but leave his wallet and everything else. He felt humiliated and scared. That Clint Peebles and Juan Martinez had taken off their masks meant that they no longer cared if he could identify them, and that was a very bad thing. He was sick about Champ.

Clint was close enough to Parker in the cab that he could smell the lawyer's fear and his morning breath. Up close, Clint noticed, the lawyer had bad skin. He'd never noticed in the courtroom.

"So, you know where we're going," Clint said.

"The Engler place," Parker said.

"That's right. And do you know what we're going to do there?"

After a long pause, Parker said, "No, Clint, I don't."

"I think you do."

"Really, I—"

"Shut up," Clint said to Parker. To Juan, he said, "There's a gate up ahead. When you stop at it, I'll get Paul here to come and help me open it. You drive through and we'll close it behind us. If you see him try anything hinky, do the same thing to him you did to that dog."

"Champ," Parker said woodenly.

"Ho-kay," Juan said.

Juan Martinez was a mystery to Parker. He'd never seen or heard of him before that morning. Martinez was stocky and solid with thick blue-black hair, and he wore a wispy gunfighter's mustache that made his face look unclean. He had piercing black eyes that revealed nothing. He was younger than Clint, and obviously deferred to him. The two men seemed comfortable with each other and their easy camaraderie suggested long days and nights in each other's company. Juan seemed to Parker to be a blunt object; simple, hard, without remorse.

Clint Peebles was dark and of medium height and build and he appeared older than his fifty-seven years, Parker thought. Clint had a hard, narrow, pinched face, leathery dark skin that looked permanently sun- and windburned, the spackled sunken cheeks of a drinker, and a thin white scar that practically halved his face from his upper lip to his scalp. He had eyes that were both sorrowful and imperious at the same time, and teeth stained by nicotine that were long and narrow like horse's teeth. His voice was deep with a hint of country twang and the corners of his mouth pulled up when he spoke, but it wasn't a smile. He had a certain kind of coiled menace about him, Parker thought. Clint was the kind of man one shied away from if he was coming down the sidewalk or standing in the aisle of a hardware store, because there was a dark instability about him that suggested he might start shouting or lashing out or complaining and not stop until security was called. He was a man who acted and dressed like a cowpoke, but he had grievances inside him that burned hot.

Parker had hoped that when the trial was over

he'd never see Clint Peebles again for the rest of his life.

Parker stood aside with his bare hands jammed into the pockets of his coat. He felt the wind bite his bare ankles above his slippers and burn his neck and face with cold. He knew Juan was watching him closely so he tried not to make any suspicious moves or reveal what he was thinking.

He had no weapons except for his hands and fists and the ball of keys he'd been ordered to bring along. He'd never been in a fistfight in his life, but he could fit the keys between his fingers and start swinging.

He looked around him without moving his head much. The prairie spread out in all directions. They were far enough away from town that there were no other vehicles to be seen anywhere, or buildings or power lines.

"Look at that," Clint said, nodding toward the north and west. Parker turned to see lead-colored clouds rolling straight at them, pushing gauzy walls of snow.

"Hell of a storm coming," Clint said.

"Maybe we should turn back?" Parker offered.

Clint snorted with derision.

Parker thought about simply breaking and running, but there was nowhere to run.

It was a standard barbed-wire ranch gate, stiff from disuse. Wire loops from the ancient fence post secured the top and bottom of the gate rail. A heavy chain and padlock mottled with rust stretched between the two. "You got the keys," Clint said, gesturing with his Colt.

Parker dug the key ring out of his pocket and bent over the old lock. He wasn't sure which key fit it, or whether the rusty hasp would unsnap. While he struggled with the lock, a beach-ball-sized tumbleweed was dislodged from a sage-brush by the wind and it hit him in the back of his thighs, making him jump. Clint laughed.

Finally, he found the right key and felt the mechanism inside give. Parker jerked hard on the lock and the chain dropped away on both sides.

"Stand aside," Clint said, and shot him a warning look before he put his pistol in his pocket and leaned against the gate. The way to open these tight old ranch gates was to brace oneself on the gate side, thread one's arms through the strands until the shoulder was against the gate rail, and reach out to the post and pull. The move left Clint vulnerable.

Parker thought if he was prepared to do something and fight back, this was the moment. He could attack Clint before Juan could get out of the pickup. He felt his chest tighten and his toes curl and grip within his slippers.

Clint struggled with it. "Don't just stand there," Clint, red-faced, said to Parker through gritted teeth. "Help me get this goddamned thing open."

Parker leaned forward on the balls of his feet.

He considered hurtling himself like a missile toward Clint, then slashing at the man's face and eyes with the keys. He could tear Clint's gun away, shoot Clint, and then use it on Juan. That's what a man of action would do. That's what someone in a movie or on television would do.

Instead, the lawyer bent over so he was shoulder to shoulder with Clint, and his added bulk against the gatepost was enough that Clint could reach up and pop the wire over the top and open it.

Back inside the pickup, they drove into the maw of the storm. It had enveloped them so quickly it was astonishing. Pellets of snow rained across the hood of the pickup and bounced against the cracked windshield. The heater blew hot air that smelled like radiator fluid inside the cab. Parker's teeth finally stopped chattering, but his stomach ached from fear and his hands and feet were cold and stiff.

Juan leaned forward and squinted over the wheel, as if it would help him see better.

"This is the kind of stuff we live with every day," Clint said to Parker. "Me and Juan are out in this shit day after day. We don't sit in plush offices taking calls and sending bills. This is the way it is out here."

Parker nodded, not sure what to say.

"The road forks," Juan said to Clint in the backseat. "Which way do we go?"

"Left," Clint said.

"Are you sure?"

"Goddammit, Juan, how many years did I spend out here on these roads?"

Juan shrugged and eased the pickup to the left. They couldn't see more than fifty feet in any direction. The wind swirled the heavy snow and it buffeted the left side of the pickup truck, rocking the vehicle on its springs when it gusted.

Parker said, "When this is over and you've got whatever it is you want, what then?"

Clint said, "I'm still weighing that one, counselor. But for now just let me concentrate on getting to the house."

"It would be helpful to know what you've got in mind," Parker said, clearing his throat. Trying to sound conversational. "I mean, since I'm playing a role in this, I can be of better service if I know your intentions."

Clint backhanded the lawyer with his free hand, hitting him hard on the ear. Parker winced.

"Just shut up until we get there," Clint said. "I heard enough talking from you in that courtroom to last the rest of my pea-pickin' life. So just shut up or I'll put a bullet into the back of your head."

Juan appeared to grimace, but Parker determined it was a bitter kind of smile.

Clint said to Parker, "You got the keys to that secret room old Engler has, right? The one he never let anybody into? The one with the books?"

● ● ●

"How far?" Juan asked. They were traveling less than five miles an hour. The snow was so thick, Parker thought, it was like being inside a cloud. Tall sagebrush just a few feet from the road on either side looked like gray commas. Beyond the brush, everything was two-tone white and light blue.

"What's in the road?" Juan asked, tapping on the brake to slow them down even further.

Parker looked ahead. Six or seven oblong shadows emerged from the whiteout. They appeared suspended in the air. They looked like small coffins on stilts.

The pickup inched forward. The forms sharpened in detail. Pronghorn antelope—part of the same herd or from another herd. A buck and his does. They stood braced into the storm, oblivious to the truck. Juan drove so close to them Parker could see snow packed into the bristles of their hide and their goat-like faces and black eyes. The buck had long eyelashes, and flakes of snow caught in them. His horns were tall and splayed, the hooked-back tips ivory-colored.

"Fucking antelope," Clint said. "Push 'em out of the way or run right over them."

Instead, Juan tapped the horn on the steering wheel. The sound was distant and tinny against the wind, but the pronghorns reacted; haunches bunching, heads ducking, they shot away from the road as if they'd never been there.

Parker wished he could run like that.

"Few miles," Clint said, "we'll pass under an archway. I helped build that arch, you know."

"I didn't know that," Parker said.

"Me and Juan," Clint said to Parker, "we've worked together for the past, what, twelve years?"

Juan said, "Twelve, yes. Twelve."

"Some of the shittiest places you could imagine," Clint said. "All over the states of Wyoming and Montana. A couple in Idaho. One in South Dakota. Most of those places had absentee owners with pricks for ranch foremen. They're the worst, those pricks. They don't actually own the places, so for them it's all about power. You give pricks like that a little authority and they treat the workingman like shit. Ain't that right, Juan?"

"*Eees* right."

Parker thought: *It's like we're the only humans on earth.* The world that had been out there just that morning—the world of vistas and mountains and people and cars and offices and meetings— had been reduced for him to just this. Three men in the cab of a pickup driving achingly slow through a whiteout where the entire world had closed in around them. Inside the cab there were smells and weapons and fear. Outside the glass was furious white rage.

There was a kind of forced intimacy that was not welcome, Parker thought. He'd been reduced to the same level as these two no-account ranch hands who between them didn't have a nickel to rub together. They had guns and the advantage, Parker thought, but they were smart in the way coyotes or other predators were smart, in that they knew innately how to survive but didn't have a clue how to rise up beyond that. He knew that from listening to Clint testify in court in halting sentences filled with poorly chosen words. And when Clint's broken-down ninety-eight-year-old grandfather took the stand, it was all over. Parker had flayed the old man with whips made of words until there was no flesh left on his ancient bones.

Clint likely couldn't be reasoned with—he knew that already. No more than a coyote or a raven could be reasoned with. Coyotes would never become dogs. Likewise, ravens couldn't be songbirds. Clint Peebles would never be a reasonable man. He was a man whose very existence was based on grievance.

"This is getting bad," Juan said, leaning forward in his seat as if getting six inches closer to the windshield would improve his vision. *Thees.*

Parker gripped the dashboard. The tires had become sluggish beneath the pickup as the snow accumulated. Juan was driving more by feel than by vision, and a few times Parker felt the tires leave the two-track and Juan had to jerk the wheel to find the ruts of the road again.

"We picked a bad day for this," Juan said. *Thees.*

"Keep going," Clint said. "We been in worse than this before. Remember that time in the Pryor Mountains?"

"*Sí.* That was as bad as this."

"That was *worse,*" Clint said definitively.

There was a metallic clang and Parker heard something scrape shrilly against the undercarriage of the truck.

"What the hell was that?" Clint asked Juan.

"A T-post, I think."

"Least that means we're still on the road," Clint said.

"*Ay-yi-yi,*" Juan whistled.

"We could turn around," Parker said.

"We could," Juan agreed. "At least I could follow our tracks back out. As it is, I can't see where we're going."

"We're fine, goddammit," Clint said. "I know where we are. Keep going. We'll be seeing that old house anytime now."

Parker looked out his passenger window. Snow was sticking to it and covering the glass. Through a fist-sized opening in the snow, he could see absolutely nothing.

He realized Clint was talking to him. "What did you say?"

"I said I bet you didn't expect you'd be doing this today, did you?"

"No."

"You're the type of guy who thinks once a judge says something, it's true, ain't you?"

Parker shrugged.

"You thought after you made a fool of my grandpa you were done with this, didn't you?"

"Look," Parker said, "we all have jobs to do. I did mine. It wasn't personal."

Parker waited for an argument. Instead, he felt a sharp blow to his left ear and he saw spangles where a moment ago there had been only snow. That voice that cried out had been his.

He turned in the seat, cupping his ear in his hand.

Clint grinned back. Parker noticed the small flap of skin on the front sight of the Colt. And his fingers were hot and sticky with his blood.

"You say it ain't personal, lawyer," Clint said, "but look at me. *Look* at me. What do you see?"

Parker squinted against the pain and shook his head slowly as if he didn't know how to answer.

"What you see, lawyer, is a third-generation loser. That's what you see, and don't try to claim otherwise or I'll beat you bloody. I'll ask you again: What do you see?"

Parker found that his voice was tremulous. He said, "I see a workingman, Clint. A good-hearted workingman who gets paid for a hard day's work. I don't see what's so wrong with that."

"Nice try," Clint said, feinting with the muzzle toward Parker's face like the flick of a tongue from a snake. Parker recoiled, and Clint grinned again.

"That man fucked over my grandpa and set this all in motion," Clint said. "He cheated him and walked away and hid behind his money and his lawyers for the rest of his life. Can you imagine what my grandpa's life would have been like if he hadn't been fucked over? Can you imagine what my life would have been like? Not like this, I can tell you. Why should that man get away with a crime like that? Don't you see a crime like that isn't a one-shot deal? That it sets things in motion for generations?"

"I'm just a lawyer," Parker said.

"And I'm just a no-account workingman," Clint said. "And the reason is because of people like you."

"Look," Parker said, taking his hand away from his ear and feeling a long tongue of blood course down his neck into his collar. "Maybe we can go back to the judge with new information. But we need new information. It can't just be your grandfather's word and his theories about Nazis and—"

"They weren't just theories!" Clint said, getting agitated. "It was the truth."

"It was so long ago," Parker said.

"That doesn't make it less true!" Clint shouted.

"There was no proof. Give me some proof and I'll represent you instead of the estate."

Parker shot a glance at the rearview mirror to find Clint deep in thought for a moment. Clint said, "That's interesting. I've seen plenty of whores, but not many in a suit."

"Clint," Juan said sadly, "I think we are lost."

The hearing had lasted less than two days. Paul Parker was the lawyer for the Fritz Engler estate, which was emerging from probate after the old man finally died and left no heirs except a disagreeable out-of-wedlock daughter who lived in Houston. From nowhere, Benny Peebles and his grandson Clint made a claim for the majority of the Engler estate holdings. Benny claimed he'd been cheated out of ownership of the ranch generations ago and he wanted justice. He testified it had happened this way:

Benny Peebles and Fritz Engler, both in their early twenties, owned a Ryan monoplane together. The business model for Engler-Peebles Aviation was to hire out their piloting skills and aircraft to ranchers in northern Wyoming for the purpose of spotting cattle, delivering goods, and transporting medicine and cargo. They also had contracts with the federal and state government for mail delivery and predator control. Although young and in the midst of the Depression, they were two of the most successful entrepreneurs the town of Cody had seen. Still, the income from the plane barely covered payments and overhead and both partners lived hand to mouth.

Peebles testified that in 1936 they were hired

by a rancher named Wendell Oaks to help round up his scattered cattle. This was an unusual request, and they learned Oaks had been left high and dry by all of his ranch hands because he hadn't paid them for two months. Oaks had lost his fortune in the crash and the only assets he had left before the bank foreclosed on his sixteen-thousand-acre spread were his Hereford cattle. He'd need to sell them all to raise $20,000 to save his place, and in order to sell them he'd need to gather them up. The payments to Engler-Peebles would come out of the proceeds, he assured them.

Benny said Fritz was enamored with the Oaks Ranch—the grass, the miles of river, the timber, and the magnificent Victorian ranch house that cost Oaks a fortune to build. He told Benny, "This man is living on my ranch, but he just doesn't know it yet."

Benny didn't know what Fritz meant at the time, although his partner, he said, always had "illusions of grandiosity," as Benny put it.

Fritz sent Benny north to Billings to buy fence to build a massive temporary corral for the cattle. While he was gone, Fritz said, he'd fly the ranch and figure out where all the cattle were.

Benny returned to Cody four days later, followed by a truck laden with rolls of fence and bundles of steel posts. But Fritz was gone, and so was the Ryan. Wendell Oaks was fit to be tied.

Bankers were driving out to his place from Cody to take measurements.

Three days later, while Benny and some locals he'd hired on a day rate were building the corral, he heard the buzz of an airplane motor. He recognized the sound and looked up to see Fritz Engler landing the Ryan in a hay meadow.

Before Benny could confront his partner, Fritz buttonholed one of the bankers and they drove off together into town. Benny inspected their monoplane and saw where Fritz had removed the copilot seat and broken out the interior divides of the cargo area to make more space. The floor of the aircraft was covered in white bristles of hair and animal feces. It smelled dank and unpleasant.

The next thing Benny knew, sheriff's deputies descended on the place and evicted Wendell Oaks. Then they ordered Benny and his laborers off the property by order of the sheriff and the bank and new owner of the ranch, Fritz Engler, who had paid off the outstanding loan balance and now owned the paper for the Oaks Ranch.

The arch appeared out of the snow and Juan drove beneath it. Parker was relieved to discover how close they were to the ranch house, and just as frightened to anticipate what might come next.

Clint was wound up. "That mean old German son of a bitch never even apologized," he said heatedly from the backseat. "He used the airplane my grandpa owned half of to swindle our family out of this place, and he never even said sorry. If nothing else, we should have owned half of all this. Instead, it turned my family into a bunch of two-bit losers. It broke my grandpa and ruined my dad and now it's up to me to get what I can out of it. What choice do I have since you cheated us again in that court?"

"I didn't cheat you," Parker said softly, not wanting to argue with Clint in his agitated state. "There was no proof—"

"Grandpa told you what happened!" Clint said.

"But that story you told—"

"He don't lie. Are you saying he lied?"

"No," Parker said patiently. "But I mean, *come on*. Who is going to believe that Fritz Engler trapped a hundred antelope fawns and flew them around the country and sold them to zoos? That he sold some to Adolf Hitler and flew that plane all the way to Lakehurst, New Jersey, and loaded a half-dozen animals on the *Hindenburg* to be taken to the Berlin Zoo? I mean, come on, Clint."

"It happened!" Clint shouted. "If Grandpa said it happened, it fucking happened."

Parker recalled the skeptical but patient demeanor of the judge as old Benny Peebles droned on at the witness stand. There were a few snickers from the small gallery during the tale.

Juan shook his head and said to Parker, "I hear

this story before. Many times about the plane and the antelopes."

Parker decided to keep quiet. There was no point in arguing. Clint spoke with the deranged fervor of a true believer, despite the outlandishness of the tale.

Clint said, "Look around you. There are thousands of antelope on this ranch, just like there were in 1936. Engler used the plane to herd antelope into a box canyon, where he bound them up. Grandpa showed me where he done it. Engler loaded them into the Ryan and started east, selling them all along the way. He had connections with Hitler because he was German! His family was still over there. They were a bunch of fucking Nazis just like Engler. He knew who to call.

"He sold those fawns for a hundred to two hundred dollars each because they were so rare outside Wyoming at the time. He could load up to forty in the plane for each trip. He made enough cash money to buy airplane fuel all the way to New Jersey and back and still had enough to pay off Wendell Oaks's loan. He did the whole thing in a plane co-owned by my grandpa, but never cut him in on a damned thing!

"Then he started buying other ranches," Clint said, speaking fast, spittle forming at the corners of his mouth. "Then they found that damned oil. Engler was rich enough to spend thousands on lawyers and thugs to keep my grandpa and my dad away from him all those years. Our last shot was contesting that old Nazi's estate—and *you* shut us out."

Parker sighed and closed his eyes. He'd grown up in Cody. He despised men who blamed their current circumstances on past events as if their lives were preordained. Didn't Clint know that in the West you simply reinvented yourself? That family legacies meant next to nothing?

"I can't take this ranch with me," Clint said. "I can't take enough cattle or vehicles or sagebrush to make things right. But I sure as hell can take that damned book collection of his. I've heard it's worth hundreds of thousands. Ain't that right, Parker?"

"I don't know," Parker said. "I'm not a collector."

"But you've seen it, right? You've been in that secret room of his?"

"Once." Parker recalled the big dark room with floor-to-ceiling oak bookshelves that smelled of paper and age. Fritz liked to sit in a red-leather chair under the soft yellow light of a Tiffany lamp and read, careful not to fully open or damage the books in any way. It had taken him sixty years to amass his collection of mostly leather-bound first editions. The collection was comprised primarily of books about the American West and the Third Reich in original German. While Parker browsed the shelves he had noted both volumes of *Mein*

Kampf with alarm but had said nothing to the old man.

"And what was in there?" Clint said. "Did you see some of the books I've heard about? Lewis and Clark's original journals? Catlin's books about Indians? A first edition of Irwin Wister?"

"Owen Wister," Parker corrected. "*The Virginian.* Yes, I saw them."

"Ha!" Clint said with triumph. "I heard Engler brag that the Indian book was worth a half million."

Parker realized two things at once. They were close enough to the imposing old ranch house they could see its Gothic outline emerge from the white. And Juan had stopped the pickup.

"Books!" Juan said, biting off the word. *"We're here for fucking books? You said we would be getting his treasure."*

"Juan," Clint said, "his books are his treasure. That's why we brought the stock trailer."

"I don't want no books!" Juan growled. "I thought it was jewelry or guns. You know, *rare* things. I don't know nothing about old books."

"It'll all work out," Clint said, patting Juan on the shoulder. "Trust me. People spend a fortune collecting them."

"Then they're fools," Juan said, shaking his head.

"Drive right across the lawn," Clint instructed Juan. "Pull the trailer up as close as you can get to the front doors so we don't have to walk so far with the—"

"So we can fill it with shitty old books," Juan said, showing his teeth.

"Calm down, amigo," Clint said to Juan. "Have I ever steered you wrong?"

"About a thousand times, amigo."

Clint huffed a laugh, and Parker watched Juan carefully. He didn't seem to be playing along.

Clint said, "Keep an eye on the lawyer while I open the front door." To Parker, he said, "Give me those keys."

Parker handed them over and he watched Clint fight the blizzard on his way up the porch steps. The wind was ferocious and Clint kept one hand clamped down on his hat. A gust nearly drove him off the porch. If anything, it was snowing even harder.

"Books," Juan said under his breath. "He tricked me."

The massive double front doors to the Engler home filled a gabled stone archway and were eight feet high and studded with iron bolt heads. Engler had a passion for security, and Parker remembered noting the thickness of the open door when he'd visited. They were over two inches thick. He watched Clint brush snow away from the keyhole and fumble with the key ring with gloved fingers.

"Books are not treasure," Juan said.

Parker sensed an opening. "No, they're not. You'll have to somehow find rich collectors who will overlook the fact that they've been stolen. Clint doesn't realize each one of those books has an ex libris mark."

When Juan looked over puzzled, Parker said, "It's a stamp of ownership. Fritz didn't collect so he could sell the books. He collected because he loved them. They'll be harder than hell to sell on the open market. Book collectors are a small world."

Juan cursed.

Parker said, "It's just like his crazy story about the antelope and the *Hindenburg*. He doesn't know what he's talking about."

"He's *crazy*."

"I'm afraid so," Parker said. "And he sucked you into this."

"I didn't kill your dog."

"What?"

"I didn't kill it. I shot by its head and it yelped. I couldn't shoot an old dog like that. I like dogs, if they don't want to bite me."

"Thank you, Juan." Parker hoped the storm wasn't as violent in town and that Champ would find a place to get out of it.

They both watched Clint try to get the door open. The side of his coat was already covered with snow.

"A man could die just being outside in a storm like this," Parker said. Then he took a long breath and held it.

"Clint, he's crazy," Juan said. "He wants to fix his family. He don't know how to move on."

"Well said. There's no reason why you should be in trouble for Clint's craziness," Parker said.

"Mister, I know what you're doing."

"But that doesn't mean I'm wrong."

Juan said nothing.

"My wife . . ." Parker said. "We're having some problems. I need to talk to her and set things right. I can't imagine never talking to her again. For Christ's sake, my last words to her were 'Don't let the door hit you on the way out.'"

Juan snorted.

"Please . . ."

"He wants you to help him," Juan said, chinning toward the windshield. Beyond it, Clint was gesticulating at them on the porch.

"We can just back away," Parker said. "We can go home."

"You mean just leave him here?"

"Yes," Parker said. "I'll never breathe a word about this to anyone. I swear it."

Juan seemed to be thinking about it. On the porch, Clint was getting angrier and more frantic. Horizontal snow and wind made his coat sleeves and pant legs flap. A gust whipped his hat off, and Clint flailed in the air for it but it was gone.

"Go," Juan said.

"But I thought—"

"Go now," he said, showing the pistol.

Parker was stunned by the fury of the storm. Snow stung his face and he tried to duck his head beneath his upraised arm to shield it. The wind was so cold it felt hot on his exposed bare skin.

"Help me get this goddamned door open!" Clint yelled. "I can't get the key to work." He handed Parker the keys.

"I don't know which one it is any more than you do," Parker yelled back.

"Just fucking try it, counselor!" Clint said, jabbing at him with the Colt.

Parker leaned into the door much as Clint had. He wanted to block the wind with his back so he could see the lock and the keys and have room to work. He tried several keys and none of them turned. Only one seemed to fit well. He went back to it. He could barely feel his fingers and feet.

He realized Clint was shouting again.

"Juan! Juan! What the hell are you doing?"

Parker glanced up. Clint was on the steps, his back to him, shouting and waving his arms at the pickup and trailer that vanished into the snow. Faint pink taillights blinked out.

At that moment, Parker pulled up on the iron

door handle with his left hand while he turned the key with his right. The ancient lock gave way.

Parker slammed his shoulder into the door and stepped inside the dark house and pushed the door shut behind him and rammed the bolt home.

Clint cursed at him and screamed for Parker to open the door.

Instead, Parker stepped aside with his back against the cold stone interior wall as Clint emptied his Colt .45 at the door, making eight dime-sized holes in the wood that streamed thin beams of white light to the slate-rock floor.

He hugged himself and shivered and condensation clouds from his breath haloed his head.

Parker roamed through Engler's library, hugging himself in an attempt to keep warm and to keep his blood flowing. There were no lights and the phone had been shut off months before. Muted light filtered through gaps in the thick curtains. Outside, the blizzard howled and threw itself against the old home but couldn't get in any more than Clint could get in. Snow covered the single window in the library except for one palm-sized opening, and Parker used it to look around outside for Clint or Clint's body but he couldn't see either. It had been twenty minutes since he'd locked Clint out.

At one point he thought he heard a cry, but when

he stopped pacing and listened all he could hear was the wind thundering against the windows.

He started a fire in the fireplace using old books as kindling and fed it with broken furniture and a few decorative logs he'd found in the great room downstairs. Orange light from the flames danced on the spines of the old books.

He wanted a fire to end all fires that would not only warm him, but also act as his shield against the storm and the coming darkness outside.

After midnight Parker ran out of wood and he kept the fire going with Engler's books. Mainly the German language volumes. The storm outside seemed to have eased a bit.

As he reached up on the shelves for more fuel, his fingers avoided touching the copies of *Mein Kampf*. The act of actually touching the books terrified Parker in a way he couldn't explain.

Then he reasoned that if books were to be burned, *Mein Kampf* should be one of them. As he tossed the volumes into the flames, a loose square of paper fluttered out of the pages onto the floor.

Parker bent over to retrieve it and flick it into the fire when he realized it was an old photograph. The image in the firelight made him gasp.

Parker ran down the stairs in the dark to the front door and threw back the bolt. The force of the wind opened both the doors inward and he squinted against the snow and tried to see into the black-and-white maelstrom.

"Clint!" he shouted to no effect. "Clint!"

AUTHOR'S NOTE

The story is fiction, but the photograph is not.

In 1936, in one of the odder episodes of the modern American West, Wyoming rancher and noted photographer Charles Belden did indeed catch pronghorn antelope fawns on his ranch and deliver them to zoos across the nation in his Ryan monoplane, including a delivery to the German passenger airship LZ 129 *Hindenburg* in Lakehurst, New Jersey, bound for the Berlin Zoo.

The photograph appears courtesy of the Charles Belden Collection, American Heritage Center, University of Wyoming.

I can find no information on the fate of the pronghorn antelope. They would have arrived shortly after the conclusion of Adolf Hitler's Olympics.

—CJB

DULL KNIFE

When it's twenty-two degrees below zero on a high mountain lake, the cracking of the ice makes an unearthly howling bellow that chills the blood and makes hearts skip a beat. The crack itself, looking like a jagged bolt of crystal-white lightning, zips across the ice with the flick of a lizard's tongue. But it is the sound of the crack, the plaintive, anguished moan, that penetrates a man and makes his skin crawl, reminding him that if the earth wanted to swallow him up, well, it could. And no one could stop it.

Wyoming game warden Joe Pickett froze with the sound and looked down at his feet as the crack shot between them. The sound washed over and through him. The crack itself was no danger to him. Ice shifted and buckled all the time. Nevertheless, he sidestepped over the crack before continuing.

The ice fishermen were still a quarter of a mile away across the surface of Dull Knife Reservoir in the Bighorn Mountains. Four fishermen, two sitting on upturned plastic buckets, two standing near their holes in the ice. All bundled up like black snowmen, their shapes rounded and without angles because of the thick winter parkas and insulated coveralls they wore. Snippets of their conversation carried crisply over the distance: a growl, a laugh, a bark. They were obviously watching him approach, and were amused when he froze and altered course.

In January, Joe had little to do besides paperwork, reports, and repairs. All of the hunting seasons were closed, and the streams and lakes were frozen. Except for a few goose hunters who had pits on the southeastern corner of his district, checking the licenses of ice fishermen was the only game in town. Even though it was nearing dusk and he could literally feel the temperature dropping as the sun gave up, defeated, and slipped behind the western mountains, he had decided to park his truck and walk across the ice to check the fishermen out. Well, not really a walk. More like a shuffle.

Joe admired ice fishermen, although he thought they were crazy. To stand around on the surface of a lake, fishing through a hole that had been augured through fourteen inches of ice, took a special breed. To fish when it was twenty-two below took a particular kind of dedication, or madness. Joe often thought that if he caught an ice fisherman without a license, the violator should be sentenced to more ice fishing for punishment.

"Hey, Joe," one of the fishermen called out. "Fine weather we're having." The other three laughed. Joe smiled. He recognized the fisherman to be Hans, a retired Saddlestring cop who now worked part-time as a janitor for Barrett's

Pharmacy. Jack, his partner for hunting and fishing, was a retired schoolteacher. The other two fishermen were their sons.

"How's fishing?" Joe asked.

Jack opened a cooler and displayed a dozen fat rainbow trout and two dozen silvery cans of beer. "Fishing's been good," Jack said. "You can make up for every fish you lost in the summer by fishing in the winter."

Joe admired the big fish, oohing and aahing. "Since I walked out all this way . . ." he started to say.

"You want to check our licenses," Hans finished for him. All four men started unzipping and unsnapping their coats, digging through layers to find their wallets.

"Do you know anything about that light under the ice over there?" Hans's son asked as he handed his license to Joe.

"What light?"

Hans pointed across the lake. "We noticed it this morning when we came out," he said. "It was still dark, and it looked like it was lit up under the ice. It was kind of creepy."

Joe looked where Hans was pointing, and he could see it. On the far shore, beneath the black wooded bluff of the shoreline, was a faint yellow glow.

"Are you sure it's not a reflection from some-where?" Joe asked.

"Where?" Hans asked back.

Joe squinted. "How could there be a light *under* the ice?"

"That's what we were wondering," Jack said. "We were going to walk over there and check it out, but the fish started hitting and, well, you know."

Joe nodded, handing back all of the licenses, but he continued to look across the lake. As it got darker, the glow became more pronounced.

Hans's son said, "Jesus, it's getting cold all of a sudden."

"We'd best head back," Jack said, reaching down to clear a skin of ice from the top of his fishing hole so he could reel in.

"Let me know what you find over there," Hans said to Joe. "I'd go with you, but my feet are starting to freeze."

"That's because you have old feet," Hans's son said, cracking open a beer.

"Not so old I can't kick your ass with one of 'em," Hans said.

Jack hooted.

Joe smiled and left.

He shuffled across the lake as the sun set. Hard white stars flickered in the sky, followed by a thin slice of moon that seemed too cold to bloom full. Joe felt icy fingers of cold probing into his collar and up his sleeves. He knew his feet would freeze, even in his thick Sorel Pac boots, the moment he stopped walking.

There was no doubt that there was light under the surface of the lake. It now illuminated the very ice he was walking on, so his feet looked like black silhouettes. It reminded him of being on a hip dance floor once when he was in college. He remembered dancing very badly on it. Another crack on the lake brought a moan that made the hair on the back of his neck stand up. The moan echoed softly back and forth across the lake.

He stopped and stared. Something was sticking up through the surface of ice in the middle of the glow; something thin, spindly, and black. His first thought was that it was a tree branch.

The surface of the ice changed as he walked. There was a rim of broken ice plates, then a slick surface. Ice told stories, Joe knew. Whatever happened could be seen and felt by examining the ice. Something had crashed through here, and the water had recently frozen back over it.

It was a frozen human hand, reaching up through the ice, not a branch. As he stood above it, he could see the body below, and the source of the glow beneath the surface: headlights. He felt his heart race as he stared, and a line of sweat broke out across his forehead, beneath his wool cap. He could see her face beneath the ice, despite the bolts of thick black hair that slowly whorled around it in the current. Her eyes were open, looking upward, her mouth set in a pout. She wore dark clothing. There was a light band of flesh between the top of her black jeans and the bottom of her coat. Her name was Jessica Lynn Antelope, and she had been a basketball star.

The story the ice told him was this:

The night before, the pickup truck that was now on the bottom of the lake had gone off the old two-track road that rimmed the bluff. It must have been going fast, he thought, to have launched this far into the lake. The truck had crashed through the ice and settled on the deep floor of the lake, with its rear end down first so the headlights pointed up. The engine was obviously killed in the water, but the battery held enough of a charge to power the lights a day later.

Jessica Lynn Antelope had been in the pickup, either as the driver or a passenger. She had attempted to swim to the surface toward the hole the truck had made. Whether she'd drowned before she froze to death would be a toss-up. Joe wondered if she realized, before she died, that her grasping hand had broken through the rapidly forming new skin of ice into the twenty-below air. As the water froze, it had trapped her arm and held it fast in its grip. Now her body swayed slowly in the current, her hair sweeping across her face in a fan dance.

He said, "Jesus," and dug in his parka for his cell phone to call the sheriff.

• • •

Joe waited in his pickup on the shore of the lake —engine running, heater blowing full blast—for Sheriff McLanahan and the tow truck to arrive. His toes in his boots burned as they thawed out. He was still annoyed at the tone of the conversation he had had with McLanahan.

"You found her, huh?" McLanahan had said with a heavy sigh.

"I think it's her," Joe had said, remembering Jessica from seeing her on the basketball court. She had gained weight since those days, her face was round, like a hubcap.

"Her mother called a few hours ago, said she hadn't shown up this morning. We always give missing person calls a few days if they come from the res, since those people vanish for days on end most of the time."

" 'Those people'?" Joe repeated.

"You know what I'm talking about," McLanahan said. "They operate on Indian time. If they say they'll be someplace at nine, there's no reason to worry until one or two. Same thing with the missing person calls. They always show up somewhere eventually, usually hungover."

"This is Jessica Antelope we're talking about," Joe said.

"I know, I know. But she hasn't played in five years. You know about her."

Joe did. He had heard. And he had seen her a

few times since. But he chose to remember her from the basketball court, when he and his daughter Sheridan would drive to the reservation simply to watch her play. Sheridan had idolized Jessica Antelope, studied her, tried to emulate her on the court. But despite Sheridan's grit and determination, she could not run as fast, pass as cleanly, or score forty points a game. Jessica had a blinding crossover dribble that compared legitimately to those of the great NBA point guards as she brought the ball down the court, and she left opponents flailing at air in her wake, and fans gasping. Joe had never seen a girl play basketball with so much natural grace and style, and neither had anyone else. Sheridan still had photos of Jessica Antelope, clipped from the Saddlestring *Roundup*, taped to her wall. Jessica had led the Wyoming Indian Lady Warriors, made up of only seven Northern Arapaho girls, to the state championship game, where they lost, 77–75, to Cheyenne, a much larger school. Jessica scored fifty-two points in the loss.

But the scouts didn't care about the loss. Jessica Antelope had been offered full-ride scholarships to over twenty universities, including Duke and Tennessee, the national powers. Instead, Jessica stayed on the reservation to take care of an ailing grandmother, she claimed. Then she gained weight, a lot of it. She drank beer and liquor with her friends. She took crystal meth, the scourge of the reservation, and was arrested for dealing it. Joe had seen her several times in the elk camps of out-of-state hunters, where she'd been hired as a camp cook. Joe suspected she was chosen for other services as well, and it pained him. Those hunters had no idea that the chubby twenty-two-year-old Northern Arapaho scrambling their eggs was once the greatest basketball player in the state of Wyoming.

Joe had heard Jessica had fallen in with Darrell Heywood and his friends on the res as well, and he hoped it wasn't true.

Joe stood on the shore of the lake with Sheriff McLanahan, two deputies, and the tow truck driver. The temperature was now thirty degrees below zero, and the exhaust from the tow truck engulfed them in a foul-smelling cloud.

"There's no way we'll get that truck out of there tonight," the driver said. "We'd have to hire divers to hook up the cable, and nobody in their right mind would come out tonight to do it."

"What about Jessica's body?" Joe asked McLanahan.

The sheriff shrugged. "She'll still be there tomorrow."

"What if there's someone else in the truck?" Joe asked, exasperated.

McLanahan shook his head. "They'll keep," he said. "They aren't going nowhere."

Joe shot him a look.

"Besides, we know who was in the truck with her," McLanahan said. "There's a guy in the clinic with hypothermia. It's her brother, Alan Antelope. He's called 'Smudge' on the res, I guess. He showed up last night—somebody dumped him at the emergency entrance and took off. He's in a coma, and hasn't said anything."

"So it was Jessica and her brother," Joe said. "Damn, what were they doing out here?"

McLanahan shrugged. "Why do Indians do anything they do?"

"Did you ever see her play basketball?" Joe asked.

The sheriff shook his head. "I heard she was pretty good," he said.

"She was the best I ever saw," Joe said.

"We used to play Wyoming Indian in high school," McLanahan said, addressing the tow truck driver more than Joe, launching into one of his stories that were always about *him*. "Those fucking Indians could run the court like there was no tomorrow. Run-and-gun, no set plays. They'd just try to run you right out of the building. They'd score ninety or a hundred points a game, but they didn't play defense so we'd score ninety against them. During time-outs they'd sit on the bench and light up cigarettes. I kid you not. Fucking cigarettes on the bench."

Joe turned away, started walking back to his

truck. He could hear McLanahan going on, the driver laughing.

"When we'd run against 'em in cross-country, they'd do the same damn thing. One of 'em ran until his heart exploded in his chest. Too much smoking and drinking. Shit, they'd have other Indians stationed at the finish line just to stop their runners so they wouldn't keep running and end up in the next county . . ."

"Darrell Heywood," Marybeth said to Joe at home in the bathroom. "You hate that guy, don't you?"

Joe was soaking in the tub, trying to thaw himself out. Feeling in his legs and arms was returning under the steaming water, but it hurt. After his teeth stopped chattering, he'd told her about finding Jessica Lynn Antelope in the ice.

Marybeth leaned against the doorway, arms crossed, wearing a thick robe. She looked well scrubbed and attractive, he thought. Her blond hair was mussed from a pillow, and her legs, what he could see of them beneath the robe, were firm and white. Sheridan and Lucy had been in bed for hours, since it was after midnight when Joe had gotten home. Marybeth had stayed up for him, reading a novel in bed.

"I don't know if 'hate' is the right word," Joe said. "I don't appreciate him. I don't like what he stands for."

"Hasn't he given hundreds of thousands to the

reservation?" Marybeth asked. "Out of some trust fund he's got?"

"Yeah," Joe said. "But I don't like his attitude. He pretends he's an Indian. No, not that. He pretends he's an Indian, but he thinks he's better than them. Am I making sense?"

"Hardly," Marybeth said with a slight smile.

"He gives them money, but he doesn't help them," Joe said. "He likes the idea of being close to the Indians because it feeds his ego. But he preys on them, is what I think. They're not stupid. He treats them like children, is what I'm trying to say. It's that he doesn't give them any credit that they're real human beings. To him, they're cartoon characters. People of the earth, or something."

Joe remembered being in a small audience a couple of years ago when Darrell Heywood gave the dedication for a new monument on the lawn of the Tribal Center. Heywood had designed the monument and, of course, paid for it. The granite obelisk was dedicated to the struggles of the Northern Arapaho and the Shoshone, who shared the reservation. The ceremony took place shortly after Heywood actually moved there, after he began growing his hair long and single-braiding it Indian-style, when he began to insist everyone call him by his Indian name, White Buffalo. Heywood's talk was rambling and self-indulgent, Joe thought, more about how profoundly he had been moved as a child when he first read about Pocahontas than about the struggles of the Northern Arapaho or Shoshone. How angry he was when he read *Bury My Heart at Wounded Knee*, how inspired after reading *Black Elk Speaks*. He confessed how he felt more connected to the Natives and their love of nature and mysticism than he ever was with his own parents. Heywood described, in fits and starts, his brief history of dropping out of college, traveling the country, participating in powwows and sun dances, the peyote-inspired vision he'd obtained that showed him he was related to his Native brothers and sisters by a psychic bloodline, how he'd found himself here, in Wyoming, *home at last*. He urged his brothers and sisters to resist the materialistic evils of the white man's culture, to not get caught in their trap of predation based on money, power, and industry. To go back to what they were, what made them special: being children of nature. Pure. Superior. Uncorrupted. He never mentioned his trust fund and inheritance, Joe recalled.

"So you think Jessica deteriorated because she hung out with Darrell Heywood?" she asked.

Joe thought for a moment. "Yup," he said.

"But that didn't put her in the lake, did it?"

"It might have been a factor," Joe said. "He's fairly well known for taking good care of his friends."

"Meaning he supplied them with alcohol and drugs," Marybeth said. "It's so sad."

"It is," Joe said. "Giving alcohol to an alcoholic makes him happy, but it doesn't help him. Buying stuff for people who won't work makes you popular, but it doesn't get them a job or any self-respect."

"Are you thawed out yet?" she asked.

He looked up. "Why? Do you have something in mind?"

Later, Joe slipped out of the bed and pulled on his robe against the cold that sliced into the house through the walls. He stood at the window, looking out at the night. He could feel the furnace working, fighting a holding action against the outside and not winning. A light snow fell, but the night was so cold that the flakes hung in the air and didn't land. He thought of the moan of the ice and Jessica's hand reaching through it toward the sky.

"That was nice," Marybeth said from bed, from somewhere beneath the quilts.

"She was the best point guard Sheridan and I have ever seen," Joe said.

At breakfast, Joe told Sheridan about Jessica Antelope.

"Who is she?" Lucy asked.

"She used to play basketball," Sheridan said, her

eyes moistening but her face holding steady. "Dad and I used to watch her."

"Was she as good as you?"

Sheridan exchanged looks with Joe. "She was a lot better," Sheridan said. "You know those pictures on my wall?"

"Oh," Lucy said, and went back to her cereal.

"Sorry, Sheridan," Joe said. He couldn't tell what she was thinking.

"If I could do what she did," Sheridan said, "I wouldn't waste my talent like that. Why didn't she keep playing, Dad?"

"I don't know. She's the only one who could answer that."

"What was wrong with her?" Sheridan asked. "Didn't she know how good she was?"

Joe couldn't answer that one, either.

He drove to Dull Knife Reservoir after breakfast and watched as divers in thick winter dry suits chopped Jessica Lynn Antelope's body out of the ice. When they pulled her free, her body was dark and limp and lay on the surface of the lake like a wet rag until the EMTs loaded her onto a gurney. Her frozen arm stuck out of the blanket like an antenna. The ambulance stayed until they could determine whether there were any more bodies.

It took half the day to hook up the pickup and winch it through the ice onto shore. The ice broke with the sound of explosives as they pulled it through.

Joe hung back, watching closely as the sheriff looked in the cab of the pickup.

"Dead men everywhere," McLanahan declared loudly, and a hush fell over the workers, EMTs, and sheriff's office personnel.

Then McLanahan reached through the broken-out side window and showed everyone an empty sixteen-ounce Budweiser can. "At least two six-packs of dead men in there," he said, nodding at the can. "The official beverage of the Wind River Indian Reservation." Everyone laughed.

Joe sighed and left the scene. He hated McLanahan's casual racism. Worse, he hated the fact that in too many instances, McLanahan was right.

On his way to the hospital, Joe called Nate Romanowski on his cell phone. Nate lived alone in a stone house on the bank of the Twelve Sleep River, where he flew and hunted falcons and lived well with no visible means of support. Joe trusted Nate even though most feared him, and Joe knew Nate was intimate with the tribal council of the reservation as well as many of the Shoshone and Northern Arapaho who lived there.

Nate had already heard about the discovery of Jessica Antelope's body.

"Did they find anyone else?" Nate asked.

"Not yet."

"That surprises me," Nate said. "I can't see Jessica and her brother out together by themselves. They were always surrounded by other people."

Joe told him what the sheriff had said about Alan.

"Smudge," Nate said, and Joe could picture him nodding.

"Why do they call him that?"

"When he was a little boy, his face was always dirty," Nate said. "His grandmother called him Smudge. It stuck, because his face is still always dirty."

"Hmm."

"I'd see if Smudge will talk to you," Nate said. "He's Jessica's only brother, although he's a real meth head. She's got a sister, too, named Linnie. I'd check to make sure she's all right. Linnie and Smudge hang out with Darrell Heywood. There might have been more than the two of them in that pickup."

"I hope not," Joe said, imagining other bodies drifting in Dull Knife Reservoir, their lifeless bodies bumping up against the thick shield of ice.

Joe strode down the hallway of the hospital, found the door with a placard on it that read ALAN ANTELOPE, and went in to find Smudge awake and alert and trembling violently.

Smudge was slight and dark and reminded Joe of a ferret. He had a huge blade-shaped nose and furtive eyes that didn't hold on Joe for more than a second. His head was abnormally small, perched on the end of a long neck like a balled fist.

"I thought you were supposed to be in a coma," Joe said, closing the door behind him.

"I wish I was," Smudge said, his voice a buzz-saw timbre. "I'm a fucking hurting unit, man."

Joe looked Smudge over, saw no wounds.

"I need something," Smudge said.

"You're withdrawing from meth," Joe said, as much to himself as to Smudge. "That's what hurts."

Smudge's face screwed up into a petulant fist. "Yeah, man, that's what hurts. Go tell the nurses I need something. They don't even know I'm here."

"They know," Joe said. "They just don't know you're awake. How long have you been conscious?"

"Shit, I don't know. Not long."

"What do you remember about getting here?" Joe asked.

Smudge thrust his fist of a face toward Joe to show his impatience. "I don't remember anything," he said.

"You don't remember being in a pickup with Jessica? Out at Dull Knife?"

Smudge sat back as if he'd been slapped. Joe

watched his eyes. Smudge was recalling something.

"We were in my truck," Smudge said slowly. "Out by the lake . . ."

"That we know," Joe said. "What else?"

Smudge shook his head. "It was dark, I know that."

Joe rolled his eyes.

"Next thing I remember, I was getting pushed out of a car in front of the hospital."

"Who pushed you?" Joe asked. "Who else was in the truck when it went into the lake?"

Smudge started to speak, then stopped himself. "Nobody. Just me and Jessica."

"So someone asked you to keep your mouth shut. You *do* remember that, then?"

"I don't know what you're talking about, man," Smudge said, shaking his head from side to side in an exaggerated way.

"Sure you do," Joe said. "Who told you to keep quiet? Who else was in the truck?"

"No one, I said. Man, could you get me a nurse?"

Joe tried not to glance at the call button hanging on a cord near Smudge's shoulder.

"I'll get you the nurse when you tell me who else was in the truck when it went into the lake."

"That's extortion," Smudge said.

"Yup," Joe said.

"I need something," Smudge said, rubbing his

arms with his hands as if killing ants that were crawling on his skin. "I need something bad."

"Your sister didn't make it," Joe said. "Remember her?"

Smudge looked up, stopped rubbing. His eyes glistened. "Jessie?"

"Yes. She tried to swim to the top, but she didn't make it."

Smudge nodded. He knew.

"She was the best basketball player I ever saw," Joe said. "My daughter worshipped her."

"Yes," Smudge said. "She was good, man."

"She was more than good," Joe said, remembering what Sheridan had said that morning. "Why didn't she keep playing?"

Smudge shrugged. It was as if Joe had asked him why Jessica liked chocolate over vanilla.

"Didn't she ever say?" Joe asked.

"Why are you asking me about her basketball?" Smudge asked angrily. "She didn't care about that so much. Why are you asking me? Get a nurse."

"Did she ever know how good she really was?"

"You white people. All you care about is how good she was at a stupid sport."

"Better than keeping her down with the rest of you, like you did," Joe said in a flash of rage.

Smudge said, "*Fuck* you! Get me a nurse. I'm dying here."

Joe was across the room before he even realized

it, his fingers squeezing Smudge's windpipe, Smudge turning red, his eyes bulging.

"Who was in that truck with you?"

Smudge told him.

"That's who I thought," Joe said, releasing him.

The door to the room flew open, an angry nurse filling it.

"What are you doing to him?" she demanded of Joe.

"I thought he was choking," Joe said, backing away, not quite believing what he had done, how angry he had been. "I think he's all right now."

It was dark, already fifteen below. Joe cruised his pickup on the gravel roads of the Wind River Indian Reservation. Less than half of the streetlights worked. Woodsmoke from the chimneys of tiny box houses refused to rise in the cold and hung like London fog, close to the ground.

He had always been taken by the number of basketball backboards and hoops on the reservation. Nearly every house had one, and they were mounted on power poles and on the trunks of trees. In the fall, during hunting season, antelope and deer carcasses hung from them to cool and age. In the summer, they were used by the children. This is where Jessica had learned how to play.

Beyond the homes, the brush grew thick and high along the river. The road coursed through it, and Joe slowed, inching his way along the road, looking for a sweat lodge he had been told was there.

When his headlights lit up the squat dome covered in hides, Joe keyed the mike on his radio and called Sheriff McLanahan.

"Knock, knock," Joe said, shoving aside the heavy elk hide that covered the doorway. A thick roll of steam greeted him, the steam smelling like burning green softwood and human sweat.

"Hey, close the frigging door!" a man shouted from inside, and a female giggled.

Joe ducked through the doorway, squatting under the low ceiling. The air was thick with steam and light smoke, so thick he could barely breathe. The only light was the flicker of the fire beneath the cast-iron pot of boiling water filled with herbs, roots, and leaves.

It took a moment for Joe's eyes to adjust, but as they did he could see the two people inside across from him. Linnie Antelope, Jessica's younger sister, naked and gleaming with the reflection of the fire, her wide young face staring at Joe, her eyes glazed over and vacant. A meth pipe sat on an upturned coffee can lid near her thigh.

Darrell Heywood was next to her, fat, white, and sweating. His long blond hair was stuck to his neck and chest with perspiration. He had no body hair.

"Joe Pickett," Joe said. "I'm the game warden."

"What the fuck is a game warden doing here?" Heywood asked. "You've got no jurisdiction on the reservation. We're a sovereign nation."

"We?" Joe asked rhetorically. "I thought you were from Connecticut."

Linnie giggled, then stifled the sound with her hand. Joe thought she looked a lot like Jessica, when Jessica was younger. But Linnie was just skinny; her arms were sticks. She didn't play basketball.

"You're breaching etiquette," Heywood said. "You don't just come into another man's sweat lodge. You must be invited in. And you aren't invited."

God, it was hot in here, Joe thought. He was already sweating beneath his heavy winter clothes.

"It's important," Joe said. "I couldn't wait for an invitation. I wanted to talk with you before the sheriff got here and took you off to jail."

He let that sink in.

Heywood had heavy cheekbones and a thick brow and bright blue eyes made brighter from the pipe. "What are you talking about?"

"You know," Joe said.

Heywood looked around the structure as if someone there could interpret for him.

"Darrell knows everything," Linnie said, her laugh a tinkle.

"Shut up, Linnie," Heywood scolded, then turned back to Joe. "The sheriff has no more jurisdiction here than you do."

"You've got a thing about jurisdiction, don't you?" Joe said. "But the sheriff is calling the tribal police. They'll be here together."

Heywood's face was red from the heat, but got even redder. "Get the hell out of here. Now."

"You just left her out there," Joe said. "She was trying to swim to the surface. In fact, her hand was sticking up out of the ice when I found her. If you'd stuck around just a few minutes longer, you might have helped her out."

Heywood just glared.

Joe said, "You made it to shore after the truck went into the lake and called one of your friends to pick you up from the pay phone in the campground. As far as you were concerned, both Smudge and Jessica went down to the bottom together."

"You're crazy, man. You can't prove that."

Linnie, though, had withdrawn from him, and was now looking back and forth from Heywood to Joe.

"Smudge must have gotten out on his own," Joe said. "I can't imagine you and your friends taking him to the hospital out of the kindness of your heart, but you couldn't just leave him there. Unlike you, he had no body fat to keep him warm. But you just left Jessica back there, didn't you?

You didn't figure she was tough enough to try and swim out, did you?"

"Look," Heywood said, "I told you to leave—"

"Is he talking about my sister?" Linnie asked, her voice high, unmodulated, unhinged.

"But you never saw her play," Joe said. "You didn't have a clue how tough she was, how talented she was. You never saw her potential. You didn't think of her that way."

"Jessica!" Linnie shrieked, flailing at Heywood, her bare palms slapping his naked skin, leaving white handprints.

"I thought she was in the truck!" Heywood yelled in self-defense, trying to ward off her blows. "There wasn't anything I could do!"

"You could have grabbed her hand and pulled her out," Joe said calmly. "You could have taken her to the hospital."

Linnie was whaling away at him now, her hands balled into fists, swinging like an eggbeater.

"Linnie . . ." Joe said.

"Damn you!" Heywood cried, backhanding her across the face. "Stop it! I was freezing and wet. Smudge drove us into the goddamn lake! There was nothing I could do!"

Linnie was thrown back, but kicked at him hard. The heel of one of her feet caught him under the heart and brought a groan.

Joe had his weapon out, finding it in the folds of his clothes. "Darrell, you're under arrest. I think the charge is officially 'reckless endangerment.' Kind of describes your whole life here, I'd say. You could have helped Jessica Antelope, but that wouldn't have fit your little movie here, would it?"

Heywood howled in response and stood up, tearing the top of the sweat lodge off, diving naked through the hole, his big body thumping on the ground outside.

It wasn't hard for Joe to follow the footprints in the snow, weaving in and out of the brush toward the river. And when Darrell Heywood began to moan, he was easy to locate.

Joe pushed through the brush.

Heywood had slipped on the ice of the river and fallen and was now stuck fast to it, his entire belly glued to the surface.

"I'm freezing here," he said between sobs. "I can't get free. I'm going to freeze to death."

Joe shuffled across the ice and squatted down in front of Heywood.

"Hey, White Buffalo," Joe said. "A real Indian would know not to run across a frozen river naked, I think."

Heywood spat, and cursed. Said, "I'm freezing to death."

"You've got a while yet," Joe said. "But it's not going to feel good when they peel you off."

Heywood sobbed, his tears freezing instantly on the ice.

Joe saw the flash of wigwag lights bouncing off the low-hanging woodsmoke, heard the sirens coming.

"You never saw her play," he said. "You didn't know what she could do."

LE SAUVAGE NOBLE
(THE NOBLE SAVAGE)

In reality, the source of all these differences is, that the savage lives within himself, while the social man lives constantly outside himself, and only knows how to live in the opinion of others, so that he seems to receive the consciousness of his own existence merely from the judgment of others concerning him.
—JEAN-JACQUES ROUSSEAU

Jimmy Two Bulls was driving Sophie's Citroën C6 fast but not well—he kept missing third gear—and each time he did it, Sophie would make a little intake of breath that, in other circumstances, he once thought cute. The dark highway was slick with greasy rain that filmed the windows and beaded on the hood. Oncoming headlights appeared with less and less frequency. The car was new and belonged to her husband.

"Do you know where we are?" Sophie asked. The car smelled of damp flowers and her scent. The drying blood on his shirt smelled ripe and metallic, reminding him of a deer hunting trip he once took with his uncle in the rain.

"No."

"I can *see* Paris," she said, gesturing toward the

massive orange smudge that defined the horizon and was always out there in the dark, looming, the band of light closed tightly on top as if by a kettle lid of storm clouds.

"So can I. But every turn I make seems to take us farther away."

"Maybe we can stop and ask someone how to get there. We took a wrong turn somewhere." Lovely accented English, filled with those swooping little girl squeaks sophisticated French women used, which sounded like erotic baby talk.

"Have you seen anyone to ask? I haven't."

They'd left the Buffalo Bill's Wild West Show forty-five minutes before. He was still wearing his quill breastplate.

He ran over something in the road that rattled the windows and made the steering wheel jerk. Whatever it was, he'd glimpsed it at the last second in the headlights, but not in time to steer around it. The object had been dark, long, tube-like, sodden.

"What was that?" she asked, alarmed.

"Don't know," he said. "A tree branch maybe." Or a cat.

"A tree branch?"

"Maybe," he said, grinning despite himself, "a human arm. It kind of looked like a human arm. My bud Fred Sitting Up ran over an arm once on the road back from a Valentine, Nebraska, beer run to the res. He didn't remember it until two days later, and by the time he said something about the arm, we found out a dozen other cars ran over it, too. It looked like a flattened dead snake by the time the cops found it. Never did hear who it belonged to."

"What are those lights ahead? They don't look like streetlights."

"They're not."

"What, then?"

"Fires. Burning cars."

"Shit!" she said, her eyes wide as she stretched back in the car seat, pressing her feet against the floor as if applying the brakes, the fine ropy muscles of her calves and thighs defining them-selves on her long bare legs.

"It always cracks me up," Jimmy said, flipping his braided hair over his shoulder, "how when things go to hell you people say 'shit' in English. 'Shit' was Marcel's last word."

"You're scaring me, Jimmy." She pronounced it *Jee-mee*.

He looked over at her and laughed bitterly. *"I'm* scaring *you?"*

She screamed, "You must turn around, Jimmy! Jimmy!" *Jee-mee! JEE-MEE!*

It was Lyle Bear Killer, Jimmy's cousin from Pine Ridge, who'd been the one who convinced him to come over with promises of good wine, good

219

wages (the Wild West Show needed authentic natives for the nightly 6:30 p.m. and 9:30 p.m. performances at Disneyland Paris), good food, and beautiful French women who wanted to have American Indian babies. Sure, Jimmy'd heard the stories but he had trouble believing them. French society women? *Married* French society women? Just for showing up in traditional dress, acting inscrutable and a little mystical, they'd take you home or to a hotel and fuck you all night long? How could this be possible?

So Jimmy applied for a Warrior-Wrangler job online even though he'd never been to war or ridden a horse except for a gray-white swayback on his grandfather's South Dakota ranch. He used the money he'd saved as a teaching assistant at Black Hills State to buy the handsome porcupine quill breastplate, outlandish fringed and beaded buckskin leather jacket, moccasins, and butter-soft deerskin pants at the Prairie Edge store in Rapid City, all the time feeling a little embarrassed, keeping his head down, the same kind of feeling he'd once had buying a package of condoms at the 7-Eleven along with a copy of *Indian Country News* he'd never read and a package of gum he'd never chew. He read and reread the emails from Lyle describing his sexual exploits in sophomoric, pornographic prose. Lyle claimed he had three illegitimate children he knew about and four "in the oven."

It took a month for Disney to send a lady out to interview Jimmy and others, to assess their authenticity, show him where to sign on the employment contract and strict Disney behavior agreement. She was enthusiastic, said, "They'll love the name 'James Two Bulls'! It's a *wonderful* name!" Even though by "they" she meant "Disney," he replaced it with the words "French women" in his mind. That night, he broke up with half-white, half-Lakota Jasmine, master's degree in women's studies, who seemed to coil up while he told her and then strike suddenly, calling him a contemptible gigolo, among other things that didn't sting as badly as he imagined they would.

"But," he said slyly, "I'll be doing some women studies of my own."

"They don't want *you,* you bastard," Jasmine spat. "They want a brainless dark-skinned buck! They want some child of nature!"

"It's just nice to be wanted," he said.

With his authentic American Indian garb in its own suitcase (along with some medicine wheels, feathers, beads, and other totems Lyle said they liked over there, and two rolls of Copenhagen chewing tobacco for Lyle and the Wild West crew), Jimmy flew Northwest Airlines from Rapid City to Minneapolis to Amsterdam to Paris in February. Lyle was at the airport to greet him.

Lyle introduced him around to the other Indians

at the show, some fellow Lakotas from Pine Ridge, a few Montana Crows, a gaggle of Wyoming Shoshones, a few too many damned haughty Nez Perce from Idaho, as well as the white cowboys from the same states plus Texas and Colorado. Most of the cast were ridiculously thankful for the Copenhagen, which was unavailable in the EU. Jimmy was assigned to feeding and cleaning up for the horses and buffalo in the stock area outside the auditorium during the day, and he did bit parts in the moodily lit religious ceremony as well as manning the chute gate for the indoor buffalo stampede. He learned to paint his face. Everyone admired his beaded buckskin jacket, even the actor who played Buffalo Bill. Since everybody wore costumes, Jimmy felt comfortable in his.

He met Sophie in March.

They worked five nights on, two nights off at the Wild West Show. Every performance, every night, was sold out with French families who wore cheap straw cowboy hats, ate chili, drank beer and wine, and whooped and hollered on cue. Jimmy shared Lyle's flat and paid half the rent. During the long gray days of winter they slept late, shopped, cooked, read, and showed up at the Wild West Show mid-afternoon, in the back, where the stock was kept and the dressing rooms were located. They usually came even on their days off, because it was the only place they knew where everyone spoke English, although a few of the Montana and Wyoming cowboys were on their second or third two-year contracts and had married French women and were learning the language. The dressing rooms for the American Indians were kept dark by choice, and either traditional flute or gangster rap played on individual CD players. The Crows smoked marijuana, having somehow convinced Disney personnel that it was part of their religion, which infuriated a couple of the cowboys who insisted, in vain, that Jim Beam was part of theirs.

Lyle schooled Jimmy. Lyle had taken several years of French in school, had a natural affinity for the language, and could understand most conversations. He chose not to speak it, though, and advised Jimmy to follow his lead. "In mixed company," Lyle said, "speak Lakota, not English. It goes over better. If you speak American English, it ruins the illusion," he said. "The French like to despise Americans. That's one reason they like *us*—they think we have a common enemy. We're pure and natural and the Americans whipped our ancestors and keep us in poverty, you know the drill. So if you open your mouth and that Black Hills State assistant English professor crap starts rolling out, you can kiss the rest of the evening good-bye."

Lyle was six years older, with a dark, fierce face

that was starting to fill into an oval. He wore his hair long, past his shoulder blades, with a bone comb in it. He'd bought the comb from a West African near the Louvre, but it looked authentic, he said. Lyle had once owned a landscaping business and been on the tribal council representing the Porcupine District, but he'd been accused of embezzlement and angrily resigned and drove to Rapid City to meet with the Disney recruiters. Later, Jimmy learned that Lyle probably did steal the money to pay off a new landscaping pickup.

"I don't know much Lakota," Jimmy said.

"Then fake it," Lyle said, "that's what I do. Remember how Aunt Alice talked? Stiff-like? Just do that. String words together. Who is gonna know?"

Jimmy smiled at the common reference. Aunt Alice used to bake him pies.

"You'll start picking up the French language soon enough," Lyle said. "It's total immersion, so it comes quicker. Until you do, I'll listen and tell you what they're saying. It's my secret weapon— I know what they're talking about, but they don't know it."

Jimmy nodded with appreciation.

"And don't smile," Lyle said. "If you smile, they'll think you're on to them and they won't want to screw you. Be inscrutable. Think *Fort Apache*. Think *Dances with Wolves*."

A general invitation arrived for a reception at the American embassy. Luckily, it was on their night off. The Nez Perce complained that the invitations *always* came on Lyle's nights off, and accused him of manipulating the schedule. Lyle shrugged. Sometimes the cowboys were invited, but not nearly as often as the Indians. This was a sore point among the cowboys.

Lyle decided on a ponytail held with a leather string and the bone comb. Jimmy braided and, with the help of a questionable Crow who seemed just a little too happy to help, added beaded extensions to his hair. Jimmy had never, in his life, taken so long to get dressed.

It was an hour by train from Disneyland to Paris. Jimmy was nervous and sweated inside his buckskin jacket. He'd never been on a train before, although he'd flown many times. It was one thing to be admired by the tourists at the show, those families wearing the straw cowboy hats with colored bands reading *Colorado, Texas, Wyoming,* or *Montana,* but it was another thing to be stared at by people on the train. When one well-dressed man came up to Lyle and handed him a five-euro note and said something in French about "exploitation by the Americans" and "cultural imperialism" and something nasty about the past president, Lyle nodded solemnly and took the money. After the man left, Lyle winked at Jimmy and grinned.

"George *Booosh*," Lyle mocked. "He's still *money*."

They emerged from the train at the station on Rue de Rivoli, the Tuileries Garden on their left and beyond them the Seine, behind them the Louvre. Ornate canyon walls of magnificent buildings on their right, the Eiffel Tower in soft focus, the top vanishing into the moist twilight mist. The sidewalks were crowded with tourists, mainly Japanese being shepherded by their tour leaders with little flags held aloft, the street choked with traffic. In the distance, sirens were braying in singsong. Jimmy was astounded, felt pummeled by the impact of the scene.

"Holy shit!" he cried.

Lyle shook his head, admonished, "Remember who you are."

They walked along the Rue de Rivoli, shouldering past gawkers and tourists, Jimmy feeling the heat of staring eyes on his jacket, both thrilled and embarrassed by the attention. Lyle was easy to follow, with the eagle feather in his hair. The braying of the sirens got louder, and both men stopped to watch a convoy of police vans, blue wigwag lights flashing, weave through the stopped traffic en route to somewhere up ahead of them. It was then that Jimmy saw the black-clad riot police hanging back barely out of view in the alley, more in dark knots within the gardens. The riot police wore helmets, Kevlar vests, shoulder pads, and carried Plexiglas shields.

"They look serious," Jimmy said.

"They aren't," Lyle said.

"What are they doing? What's going on here?"

Lyle stopped, turned, looked Jimmy in the eye with disdain. "This fucking place is about to blow up, is all I know."

"Who is rioting?"

Lyle shrugged. "Everybody. I can't keep track."

Jimmy looked up to see dozens of police surge from a side street, most back-stepping with their shields up, forming a gauntlet for hundreds of shouting demonstrators who poured through the passage, stopping traffic. The demonstrators were young, exuberant, dressed in grunge-like college clothes—hooded sweatshirts, denim, track shoes. They looked American, Jimmy thought, like students in his classes at Black Hills State. Many waved hand-painted signs.

"Students this time," Lyle said, "just students. The big stuff won't happen till later this summer, when all the North Africans in the suburbs get going."

A small phalanx of boys bull-rushed several policemen, stopping just short of confronting them.

"Why don't the cops bust their heads?"

"They don't do that here," Lyle said, shrugging with his palms up. "They're *tolerant*. At least that's what they call it."

Two males broke from the demonstration and got past the police, headed straight toward Lyle and Jimmy. The Lakotas stood their ground, although Jimmy felt himself start to pucker up as the boys approached.

"*Solidarité! Solidarité!*" the scruffier of the two boys said, grasping Jimmy's hands in his, thrusting his face into Jimmy's face, shaking his hands as if they were long-lost friends. "*Unité!*"

"*Solidarité*," Lyle said, mangling the word, stepping forward and raising his clenched fist high. "We are rebels!"

"Rebels!" the scruffy boy shouted back, letting go of Jimmy, raising his own fist. Then turning to the demonstrators to show off his two new friends, shouting "*Solidarité!*" which pleased them all, eliciting cheers so loud even a few of the police-men looked over their shoulders to see what had caused it.

"*Ni glasses toki ye he*?" (Where are my glasses?) Jimmy said stoically in Lakota, words he recalled clearly from Aunt Alice. "*Ni* TV Guide *toki ya he*?" (Where is my *TV Guide*?)

Both boys turned to Jimmy with reverence, as if they'd heard wisdom from an oracle.

Jimmy said in Lakota, "*Tunkasina nite oyuzune ciya!*" (Grandfather hurt his hip!)

The boys nodded solemnly and raised their fists.

Jimmy and Lyle stood on the corner with their fists raised also, shouting "Rebels!" until the boys rejoined the demonstrators, who flowed into the gardens surrounded by accommodating police-men. When they were gone, Lyle looked over, said, "That was fucking brilliant, Jimmy. Did you see how they looked at you?"

"Like they would follow me anywhere," Jimmy said.

"You're gonna be all right," Lyle said, clapping Jimmy on the shoulder and checking his wrist-watch. "We're late," he said.

As they crossed the street, Jimmy asked, "What was that all about?"

"The one thing I've learned over here," Lyle said, "is it doesn't matter what it's about as long as we cheer them on and say we're rebels just like them. It's all about being a rebel. Every-fucking-body here is a rebel. And it doesn't hurt to be Indian—that gives us street cred."

Jimmy laughed, mainly out of relief, still proud of his Lakota phrases.

Three of the female demonstrators had not crossed the street into the Tuileries, but stood on the opposite corner, giggling, shooting long looks at them. Jimmy thought they were attractive, and nudged Lyle.

"I see 'em," Lyle said. "We can do better."

They left the disappointed girls on the corner. Jimmy tried hard not to look back.

"This place . . ." he said.

"Yeah," Lyle said.

● ● ●

The American embassy on Rue Boissy d'Anglas was a fortress, Jimmy thought, with concrete barriers keeping both pedestrians and motorists away as well as a tall wrought iron fence topped with gold-painted spear tips. Inside the fence, in the foliage, U.S. Marines in desert camo stood under wall-mounted cameras and held M16s and didn't smile.

"That's not it," Lyle said, leading Jimmy on. "We're going to the Talleyrand around the corner." Which was also behind concrete barriers and rimmed with marines and cameras.

"We got this place after the war," Lyle whispered to Jimmy as they stood in a line where a marine checked invitations and IDs. "The Germans used it. There's still Nazi shit in the basement, like those guys just walked out."

"How do you know that?"

Lyle smiled. "A nice lady took me down there once. We did it on a desk. It was weird, though, because I remember looking up and seeing this calendar in German that was turned to June 1944."

"You're kidding."

"I am not. It takes a while for history to grow here."

"That makes no sense, Lyle."

"Stick around and you'll see what kind of sense it makes," Lyle assured Jimmy.

They went individually through a massive cage-like turnstile, then a metal detector, then a hand search and document check. The older marine handed Lyle's passport back to him, said, "Good seeing you again, Lyle. I see you brought along fresh meat this time."

"My cousin Jimmy," Lyle said, nodding.

The marine looked Jimmy over, assessing him, made Jimmy feel naked.

"What would you do if the ambassador stopped inviting you to these things for local color?"

"Go home, probably."

"I wish those dollies liked marines the way they like Indians."

"Ha!" Lyle said. "No chance of that."

The reception was in a high-ceilinged room dominated by hanging crystal chandeliers that glowed with gold, syrupy light. Massive windows framed the Eiffel Tower, its girders flashing with lights signaling the top of the hour. The Place de la Concorde was across the street, the Avenue des Champs-Elysées to the northwest, headlights streaming through and around the Arc de Triomphe. Jimmy had never in his life been in a space so intricate, ornate, or intimidating. The crowd was well dressed, speaking French, plucking glasses of champagne from trays carried by men and women wearing black and white. Jimmy stood with Lyle in the very back of the room, watching, acting serious and regal the way Lyle had instructed.

Jimmy began to reach for a glass from a passing waiter but Lyle stopped him. "Indians look stupid drinking champagne," Lyle hissed. "It ruins the effect. Ask for a beer or something."

Jimmy shot a look at Lyle, but withdrew his hand.

The American ambassador, who introduced himself in English and French as Bob Westgate, former congressman from San Diego, welcomed everyone and introduced tourism representatives from the states of Idaho, Wyoming, South Dakota, and Montana, the reason the reception was held.

"Tourism people," Lyle said softly, not looking over at Jimmy. "There's a parade of 'em that come over here, one after the other. Ambassador Bob hosts them and invites French travel industry people and government types. It makes for real good picking."

Jimmy didn't need to be told because he couldn't take his eyes off a tall dark-haired woman with pale skin, flashing green eyes, and dark red lipstick. She was sipping a glass of champagne and talking with a curvy redhead in a shimmering black cocktail dress, the white orbs of her breasts straining against the tight fabric. The redhead gestured toward Lyle, said something in French, and both women nodded and smiled knowingly.

"Gabrielle le Peletier," Lyle said. "She's mine."

"Which one is she?"

"Redhead."

"Who is the other?"

"I've never seen her before. You want her?"

Jesus yes, he thought. "It can't be as easy as that."

"You'll see," Lyle said.

"Do we go over and introduce ourselves? Grunt at them?"

"Naw, we just wait. They'll come to us."

"You're kidding."

"If they don't, some other babes will. Just remember who you are."

Jimmy snorted. "Who am I?"

"Don't start that," Lyle said, an edge in his voice.

While speeches were given to bored applause—the white Americans seemed so eager to please and out of place among these sophisticates, who knew how to dress, knew how to cut their hair, knew how to stand, knew they were the best-looking fish in the aquarium, Jimmy thought—his eyes left the tall woman only to check out what was going on outside. The student demonstrators they'd encountered earlier were still in the Tuileries Garden, and the crowd had tripled in size. So had the number of riot police. Police on horseback now circled the perimeter of demonstrators but kept their distance. Every few minutes, there was a surge in the crowd toward a cordon of police, and Jimmy could see the police retreat for a moment in their lines, shields glinting in the streetlights, then slowly push the demonstrators back.

He realized he seemed to be the only person in the room focusing on what was going on outside.

"I would think," Jimmy said, "they would be at the windows watching. I mean, there's a riot right out there in front of us. Don't they care?"

Lyle shook his head, but didn't look at Jimmy, said, "They pretend they can't see it."

"Why?"

"You'd have to ask them. It's like if they don't see what's going on, it isn't really happening."

Then Lyle turned, his face dark with anger. "Are you gonna keep asking questions and wasting our time, or are you gonna give some French woman a ride? Make up your fucking mind, because you're cramping my style, Jimmy."

"Sorry, Lyle."

"Get ready," Lyle said, "the reception is winding down. Meaning it's showtime."

"Don't talk," she said in English, placing her elegant fingers to his lips.

They were in a third-floor apartment four blocks from the Talleyrand. She'd led him there by the hand. The doorman nodded to her with respectful recognition and stepped aside to let them in. She inserted a key into the lock on the door and opened it but didn't turn on a light. He hesitated on the threshold for a moment until she had said, "*Entrez vous.*"

He wore nothing but the quill breastplate she insisted he keep on. In the muted blue light from the bedroom window, her skin was so white it was translucent. She was lithe and long-limbed, her legs toned by walking, he supposed. He could see the blue veins beneath her skin on her small pert breasts and abdomen. Before they went to bed, she inspected him, running her hands over his shoulders, belly, buttocks, thighs, giving his biceps a little squeeze as if checking out the freshness of a baguette.

The contrast between his light brown skin and her paleness struck him when they were pressed together, reminded him of mayonnaise on rye bread. Her skin looked like it had never seen the sun. She was the whitest woman he'd ever been with. She didn't want to play, kiss, or caress. She wanted to be taken, and responded with encouraging mewls the more aggressively and selfishly he performed. He pretended he was in control.

Her name was Sophie Duxín, and when he exploded inside her the first time she took a sharp, sweet intake of breath.

At four in the morning she stood at the window, a naked silhouette against the sheer curtains, said, "You must go now," without turning to look at him in the bed.

He was ready, but confused. "Is everything okay?"

She turned, smiled; he could see the whiteness of her teeth. "Everything is okay. Three times, that is very good." She patted her belly as she said it.

He was sore. "This apartment . . ."

"My husband owns it. He owns lots of flats."

"And he doesn't mind?"

"He doesn't know."

Jimmy felt hungover, although he hadn't drunk anything. He wished he had something now, though.

"But—"

"Don't talk," she said again, crossing the floor to him, again pressing her fingertips to his lips.

"We have an understanding," she said, looking away. "Actually, we do not." It took him a moment to understand she was referring to her husband.

She watched him dress with cool, appraising eyes. As he pulled on his beaded jacket, he said, "What does he do, your husband?"

"He's a businessman and politician," she said, sighing. "He is very well known. He works in the government. But we won't talk about him again."

"Okay," he said, wanting to know more but not wanting to risk her anger.

"I will see you in three weeks," she said, rubbing her flat belly. "By then I will know. I'll contact you."

He didn't ask, *Know what?*

She was done with him and he was exhausted and felt oddly hollow. He wanted to leave, but he also wanted to ask:

Where is he, your husband?
What would he think of what we just did?
What would he think of me?
Do you have other children?
Where do you live?
When will I see you again?
Why an Indian? Why an Indian child? Why me?
But she said, "Don't talk."

In mid-April there were hints of spring, and several days of cloudless but pure sunshine that seemed to fill Jimmy up like red meat. He'd not realized how the endless gray days had beaten him down until the sun came out. He was sitting on a bench in a small park near their apartment building, reading a note from Sophie in the sun, when Lyle joined him wearing sunglasses.

"That from her?" Lyle asked.

"She wants to see me again," Jimmy said, charmed by the way she'd written the note in English, not her language, the way she'd drawn out the block letters. He wondered who had helped her.

Lyle shook his head, lit a cigarette, blew out the smoke in a long stream. "You're doing this wrong, Jim. The point isn't to get all monogamous. The point is to spread your love around, baby." He said it with a flourish. "You understand what I'm saying?" Lyle asked.

Jimmy grunted.

"This town's filled with French women who want to have little Jimmys, little children of nature. Why deny them?"

He wasn't sure how to answer, and knew Lyle wasn't the type who wanted to hear what he was thinking, which was a combination of his carnal desire to see her again and a leaden realization that she could do him harm if he got too close.

"Might as well go," Lyle said. "Just don't be shooting blanks. That'll really piss her off."

"You think that's why she wants to see me, then?" Jimmy said.

"Why else?" Lyle said.

Sophie met him at the Champs-Elysées Clemenceau station, wearing a scarf and large sunglasses and she seemed very happy to see him. The moment he touched her hand, to give it a little hello squeeze, he felt her cool electricity shoot through him and it made his toes curl in his boots.

She told him they couldn't go back to the apartment again, they were going to another place that was "not in such a nice neighborhood."

"It is Gabrielle's," Sophie said. "She gave me a key."

He asked why they didn't go back to her husband's apartment, and she answered by dismissing the question with a wave of her hand.

They walked a long way and were soon virtually alone on the sidewalk. Jimmy noticed the decline in the appearance of the buildings from the area around the station, and the lack of people. He saw several hand-painted signs in French and Arabic.

"Not so nice," she said.

They turned a corner and he saw four Middle Eastern men in their twenties on the sidewalk coming at them smoking cigarettes, chattering. One barked a laugh at something another said.

Jimmy felt her clamp down on his hand, practically pull him across the street to the other sidewalk. He didn't like being steered like that, as if he were running away.

The men certainly noticed, and one of them said something that made the others laugh. Jimmy didn't know the words, but could read the tone and body language. They thought he was a coward for avoiding them like that. So he stopped, fixed his stare on them as they cruised down the sidewalk across the street.

"Jimmy, no," Sophie whispered urgently.

He shot a glance at her. She was scared, the skin pulled back on her face in a way that seemed to flatten it against her skull.

The men were now adjacent to them, talking among themselves, staring back at him with fixed grins on their faces. All were unshaven, with shocks of dark hair, dark eyes. Jimmy heard the words "cowboys and Indians" clearly amid the Arabic. He felt a little tremble in the inside of his legs.

In a moment, they were past. Sophie tugged hard on his arm, and he gave in when the men were far enough away to not make it look like a retreat. He wondered what he would have done if they had come at him. He was confident he would have lost. He was no fighter, and vowed to buy a knife or a gun, some kind of weapon.

In Gabrielle's apartment, Sophie said he was "brave and foolish," which he took as a compliment.

Then she stepped up to him and kissed him lightly for the first time, and took his hand and pressed it against her breasts. He liked that.

Then, deliberately, she moved his hand down until it covered her belly.

"I hope our baby is brave and foolish, too," she said.

"You mean . . . ?"

"*Oui. Merci beaucoup.*"

Which sounded to Jimmy like "good-bye," although they had sex again but it was different. She was clearly going through the motions, waiting for him to finish, her hands no longer grasping at him, pulling him in, but placed on his back because she had no place else to put them. He pretended not to notice. Afterward, while she sprawled back and he caught his breath, he shifted in the bed and lay his head on her belly. When he did, he felt her stomach muscles tighten.

She said, "No," and wriggled away.

"I wanted to try and hear the baby," he said.

She shook her head with distaste. He wondered if he had offended her in some way.

"I don't like that," she said, in explanation.

He sat up, the moment over. "I have to ask you something," he said. "Why me?"

"It's not about you. It's about my husband."

"I don't understand."

She shook her head as if to say, *Of course you don't understand.*

"Tell me," he said.

"*Non.* It's time for you to go."

As he dressed he said, "When do I get to see you again?"

She clucked at him and shooed him out the door.

That night, Jimmy had a dream that he and his son were fishing on Rapid Creek on a bright sunny day in early fall, catching firm, colorful rainbow trout on grasshopper flies. His son was dark like him but had Sophie's long limbs, delicate features, and full mouth. Jimmy had to put his rod down and untangle his son's line from bushes and branches while his son chattered at him in French and Lakota but not English, and Jimmy could understand every word.

"You're a good boy," Jimmy said, rubbing his son's head.

The boy said, *"He tuwa Ina he?"* (Who is my mother?)

"Don't be such a dumb fuck," the cowboy said to Jimmy before taking a long pull of red wine from a bottle and handing it to Lyle. "You don't want to see her again. Believe me, it's for the best."

"Yeah," Lyle said, accepting the bottle, "don't be such a dumb fuck."

It was after midnight and the stock was fed and watered and all of the customers had cleared the area although a few stragglers still wandered through the rides and exhibits. Lyle, Jimmy, and a cowboy from Montana also named Lyle sat on hay bales in the dark as a mist began to fall. They were on their third bottle.

"Believe me," Lyle from Montana said, "I been over here going on seven years. I married into them, for Pete's sake. I even speak pretty passable French. But I'll never be inside. They don't let you in. You're either French or you ain't. That's what folks don't understand."

Lyle said, "Listen to what the cowboy says, Jimmy."

"I mean, I sort of *amuse* 'em," Lyle from Montana said, "Monique's relatives, and all. But it ain't like America, where you can choose to be an American and, by God, you're an American. It don't matter what you do here, you can *never* be French."

"I don't want to be French," Lyle said. "I just want to fuck their women."

Lyle was on a roll, said, "I don't even think they like each other very much, is the goofy thing. They turn on each other like goddamned coyotes all the time. But I think the thing is they hate everybody else even more."

Jimmy said, "I really felt something with her. I think she did, too. Especially that first time."

Lyle moaned and rolled his eyes. Lyle from Montana looked away.

Lyle said, "She was fucking herself through you. Take it for what it's worth."

Lyle from Montana said, "Hell, yes."

Jimmy didn't want to discuss it further with either Lyle. And he certainly didn't want to tell them about the dream he kept having.

"Maybe you should go home," Lyle said.

"Maybe I should," Jimmy said angrily.

"I thought you were the smart one," Lyle said. "Guess not."

"Boys," the cowboy said, slapping the thighs of his Wranglers and standing up, "I think it's time for me to hit the trail."

Sophie and Gabrielle were at the next reception at the American embassy, this one for the states of Oklahoma and Texas, whose guests frustrated

Jimmy and Lyle by bringing a few of their own Indians, Cherokees.

"We ought to take those Cherokees downstairs and kick their asses," Lyle said, glowering. "Look. Gabrielle is flirting with one of them, the way she keeps sashaying past him, fluttering her eyes. What a cow."

Jimmy was wearing his beaded jacket, drinking a beer (he and Lyle had decided beer was an okay drink image-wise, as long as they didn't pour it in a glass), trying not to stare at Sophie. She refused to acknowledge him, and he was hurt and angry.

"Leave it be," Lyle said. "You had your fun. Move on."

"I can't just move on."

"The hell you can't."

"I can't," Jimmy said, putting the beer aside and striding toward her.

As he approached her, she turned her head to him, her eyes warning him off behind a frozen smile.

"Sophie . . ."

"Hello," she said, reaching out to shake his hand, her eyes telling him to leave. "Nice to meet you," she said in English. Her casual dismissal enraged him, and he squeezed sharply on her hand, but she didn't react.

"Please meet my husband," she said through gritted teeth, but still with the smile. "Marcel. Marcel?"

A compact, stocky, dark man turned from another guest. Jimmy let go of her hand, but not fast enough that Marcel didn't see the hard exchange. The next second told Jimmy everything.

Marcel's eyes flashed from Jimmy's hand to Jimmy's face and clothes, then to Sophie, to her stomach, then back to Jimmy—where they hardened into cold black stones.

He knew everything except who it had been, Jimmy thought. And now he knew *that*.

Although conversations continued, champagne was drunk, and Ambassador Bob Westgate tapped the microphone to introduce his new guests, for Jimmy the world had suddenly shrunk and become superfluous and the only people in it were Sophie, Marcel, and his son, imprisoned inside her.

Sophie looked scared, as she had when they engaged the Middle Eastern men. She put her hand on Marcel's arm. He shook it off violently, and she recoiled.

So this was about *him,* Jimmy realized. A way to spite him or get his attention. It was never about Jimmy, or Jimmy and Sophie. And maybe not about the baby, either.

Marcel took a step toward Jimmy, closing the space between them. He was four inches shorter than Jimmy, but his aura of malevolence more than made up for the difference. In a guttural voice, he ripped off a stream of words in French that reminded Jimmy of canvas tearing. Jimmy didn't know the words, but he knew he'd been threatened.

Jimmy growled back, in Lakota, "*Micinksi, tapi tonikja je?*" (Son, how is your liver?)

Which made Marcel flinch, step back, and glare at Jimmy with unmistakable surprise.

And Sophie turned her attention from Marcel to Jimmy to Marcel to Jimmy. She didn't step between them, but stayed at Marcel's side. Making her choice.

Marcel eventually worked up a kind of superior, heavy-lidded smirk, grasped Sophie's arm, and led her out of the room. Jimmy watched, his heart thumping so hard he wouldn't have been surprised if his breastplate rattled, hoping Sophie would look back over her shoulder at him. When she did he saw in her eyes not reassurance but a look that shocked and scared him: pity, disgust.

"Wow," Lyle said, suddenly next to him, "I think I know who he is now. He's some kind of famous politician or gangster. I've seen him on TV. And I think he said you're a dead man. Man, she played *you,* didn't she?"

"I don't understand," Jimmy said.

"You never will. They live in their own little world, these people. I've tried to tell you that, dude."

For the next two weeks, Jimmy didn't leave their apartment except to go to the Wild West Show with Lyle and two cowboys who picked them up. Through the window, he watched leaves pop from buds on branches like green popcorn, felt the city turn from skeletal to lush, full, and shadowed. The bite vanished from the air and was replaced by sultry warmth and Parisian light that seemed more like set design than nature.

He used Lyle's computer to find out more about Marcel Duxín, and although he couldn't read the language, what he found justified his self-imposed exile. Marcel had been involved in some kind of sex and public works kickback scandal in 1999. Newspaper photos showed him in a coat, tie, and handcuffs, being led from a building with the same smirk he'd turned on Jimmy. A trial, another scandal involving the judge and some high-administration officials (she'd said he "worked with the government"), his release. Another investigation in 2003, another arrest, same result. Something about Marcel Duxín, either what he did or who he knew, made him untouchable, like Al Capone. Jimmy couldn't understand, but he really didn't need to. As Lyle said, it was some-thing very French.

Also very French, Jimmy thought, was how much more prominence Marcel's scandals got in the newspaper than the disturbances, riots, and rising crime in the suburbs of Paris. Those things were relegated to back pages.

He found himself thinking about Sophie.

Lyle said, "Are you gonna go home?"

"No. Not yet."

"What's keeping you? That Sophie?"

"Yes."

"Anything else?"

"The baby."

Lyle struck his forehead with the heel of his hand.

Jimmy said, "It's different, Lyle. I thought we were making Indian babies for French women who loved and wanted them, showed them off. I don't trust this guy Marcel not to do something bad to that baby. Or to Sophie."

Lyle was exasperated, said, "This isn't your business. This isn't even your country."

"It's my responsibility."

"Idiot. It's *her* baby. It's *their* baby, I hate to tell you. You boned her, is all."

"I keep having these dreams, Lyle."

Lyle's face was dark with anger, his eyes bulged. He wanted to say more, but turned, grabbed a jacket from the back of the couch, said, "I'm going out. I gotta get me some air." Slammed the door before Jimmy could point out Lyle had taken Jimmy's jacket by mistake.

Lyle wasn't back in time to catch a ride to the Wild West Show with the cowboys. Jimmy expected to see him there, and looked for him all the way to showtime.

After the 9:30 performance, Jimmy was

brushing down the horses in the corrals with a currycomb when three police officers came backstage. He saw them talking to Buffalo Bill, then one of the haughty Nez Perce. He saw the Nez Perce point at him, and lead the police his way.

"They're looking for James Two Bulls," the Nez Perce said, shaking his head. "They say they found your bloody jacket by the river with your Disney ID badge in the pocket. They think you got into something with some Arab guys. You want to set them straight?"

Jimmy thought, *Marcel*.

Lyle's bloated body kissed the milk chocolate surface of the Seine River two days later. The police who escorted Jimmy to the morgue to identify his cousin didn't speak English. The only thing Jimmy could understand was they thought Lyle had wandered into the wrong neighborhood.

Which is what he told Lyle's mother when he called her.

Afterward, he called the airline to make a reservation home. Due to a general strike, there was no availability for a week, and even that was subject to last-minute change.

He told no one he was leaving. Or that he'd booked reservations for two.

Then he stole letterhead stationery and sent two tickets to Buffalo Bill's Wild West Show with backstage passes to Monsieur and Madame Duxín courtesy of the Walt Disney Company.

He tried not to look at them, tried not to stare. They sat in the front row in the dark, wearing straw cowboy hats with green bands that read *Wyoming*. Marcel seemed to be enjoying himself immensely, cheering when he was supposed to, calling for more and more wine from the waitresses. Sophie looked wary, and despite his face paint, Jimmy was sure she recognized him during the mystical ceremony act. The test would be if she turned to her husband and pointed him out. She didn't.

Jimmy watched from the shadows of the stock entrance as Annie Oakley did her trick-shooting. The audience loved her. When it came time to select an audience member to fire at targets, she selected Marcel. Jimmy had arranged it with her. Spotlights found Marcel, and the rest of the crowd cheered him on. Buffalo Bill helped him into the sandy arena, joked in French about "not shooting any of the performers in his Wild West Show," and Marcel hammed it up in the limelight, clowning with exaggerated gestures and pretending to reach into his jacket for his own gun instead of taking the rifle filled with blanks. He blew a kiss to Sophie, who responded with a frozen, cadaverous grin.

"Have you ever fired a gun before?" Annie asked over the speakers.

"*Oui*," Marcel said, winking at her, "many times!"

"Ooooh," Annie said, pretending to be impressed.

Marcel gave her a kiss on the cheek, and acted as if he were going to squeeze her buttocks. The crowd howled. Sophie looked mortified.

Marcel fired the blanks and the targets exploded by remote control. Annie pretended to be impressed, and escorted Marcel from the arena. He waved to the crowd like a soccer player who'd scored the winning goal.

Jimmy stepped back into the shadows as Annie led Marcel past him, thanking him in French for being such a good sport and saying he would receive a special marksmanship certificate with his name on it. She had him write out his name on a slip of paper, and told him to wait a moment while she delivered it to the calligrapher.

Jimmy took no chances, thinking Marcel could very well have a gun beneath his jacket, and hit the man as hard as he could in the back of the head with a Sioux war club. The sound it made was a hollow *pock,* and Marcel staggered forward, crashing against the wooden chute panels. Jimmy threw the club aside, opened the gate, and shoved Marcel inside and closed it. Just in time for Buffalo Bill's announcement, in the arena, that "the scariest thing that can happen out on the plains is when the buffalo *stampede!*"

On cue, the arena lights went off. Fake lightning crackled. Children screamed. And forty-eight buffalo came thundering down the chute, their hooves shaking the earth beneath Jimmy's feet. And as he did twice a night, he slammed back the steel chute gate to the arena to let them out. He thought he heard Marcel moan, *"Merde"* (*shit*), seconds before the herd stomped him into the sand. Blood flecked Jimmy's shirt and hands.

Sophie came backstage before the buffalo stampede act was over, showing her pass to the man guarding the door, telling him, Jimmy assumed, that she was looking for her husband.

The first thing he noticed about her when she came into the area was the diamond necklace and diamond ring, a huge one, the biggest he'd ever seen up close.

"Jimmy," she said, gesturing through the room. "Marcel?"

"He's gone."

She looked at him, puzzled.

Jimmy raised his hands so she could see the blood. "Gone," he said bitterly. "Did you forget who I was?"

She gasped, fist to her mouth, her eyes wide. She staggered back.

"Come with me," Jimmy said, leading her down the length of the chute, through the corrals, into the sultry night. She stumbled in her fine shoes in the muck of the corrals, so he kept a tight grip on her elbow so she wouldn't fall.

"Which one is yours?" Jimmy asked as they entered the VIP parking area. She stopped at the gleaming white Citroën C6.

"He's been spending some money on you, I see," Jimmy said, opening the door for her and firmly helping her onto the passenger seat.

They roared out of the parking lot into the night, raindrops on the windshield, puddles on the road that he shot through.

"Are you going to kill me, too?" she asked in that baby-talk French.

"Non."

"What will you do?"

"As long as you're carrying my baby," Jimmy said, "I'll take care of you. After that, you're on your own, lady."

She shook her head violently, either not understanding or not wanting to understand.

"We're going to America," he said. "South Dakota. You can live with me and my mom until the baby comes. Then to hell with you. You can come back here, or get a job in a whorehouse in Deadwood . . . I don't care. I don't want my baby born here or to be with you in this place I don't understand."

"Jimmy, no . . ." she whined.

"I've got two tickets for a flight tomorrow from

Charles de Gaulle. We can go to your house and you can pack tonight."

"I'm not leaving," she said defiantly.

"Sure you are."

"No!"

He would have backhanded her pretty mouth if she wasn't with child. His child.

"So old Marcel decided to start paying attention to you, huh? Is that what this was about?"

She clammed up and stared out the window.

"You don't understand my English?"

She refused to answer him.

"You got pregnant so you could show *him,* huh? And not just any kind of baby, either. A child of nature, to show what a *rebel,* what a free spirit you are. Was that it?"

He realized that in his rage he had taken several turns and exits and was now on a secondary highway. He saw a sign for Champs-sur-Marne, another for Lagny-sur-Marne.

"I don't know where we are," he said.

"The baby," she said, "we got rid of it."

He didn't react. Kept driving, increasing his speed, trying to pretend he didn't hear what she'd said. Hoping he had heard her wrong.

"Jimmy," she said, "the baby is gone."

"So that's why he bought you this," Jimmy said calmly, dead calm, caressing the dashboard of the new car, "and the jewelry. You made a deal with him, then?"

"A deal?" she said, curling her lip.

"Boy or girl?"

"Oh, Jimmy, no . . ."

"Boy or girl?"

"I don't know," she said. Then: "It was for the best."

"My son might not agree," Jimmy said.

Sophie seemed to be burrowing into the passenger door, keeping as far away from him as she could. Her eyes were on him, cautious, scared, waiting to see what he did.

"Jimmy, don't be angry," she said.

"I'm not angry," he said, a cold tumor growing exponentially in his chest. "I understand. I come from a broken nation, too, the Lakota nation. That's what we have in common, Sophie, the only thing. We're both on the wrong side of history. The only difference is you can't see it."

"You're scaring me, Jimmy." She pronounced it *Jee-mee*.

He looked over at her and laughed bitterly. "I'm *scaring* you?"

She screamed, "You must turn around, Jimmy! Jimmy!" *Jee-mee! JEE-MEE!*

He read the sign as they passed it: Clichy-sous-Bois. No Man's Land. She had seen it, too, screamed again for him to turn around.

But too late. Stunted trees gave way to low-slung buildings on both sides, broken windows,

Arabic graffiti on the plaster walls illuminated by the flames of burning cars.

Jimmy hit the brakes and swung around the charred skeleton of a tiny car, clipping it with a fender, slowed down before he plowed into a large group of people in the middle of the street who had appeared from nowhere.

"Don't stop," she screamed. "Go!"

He stopped as the group closed in around the car, the white Citroën with the now-damaged fender. He saw dark faces in the undulating fire-light, second-generation Arab faces, men and boys of the night in a suburb the police wouldn't even enter, the men dressed in the same kind of grunge clothes the college demonstrators had worn, probably their hand-me-downs.

The car began to rock. Sophie screamed. A back window smashed in, spraying glass across the seat and floor. Someone kicked the passenger door. Gobs of spittle hit the windshield.

"*JIMMEE! JIMMEE!*" she screamed. "*Go! Drive!*"

Instead, he hit the button that unlocked the doors.

"They don't want me," he said to her as they opened the door, dragged her out, brown hands gripping her white arms. She kicked out, threw a spike-heeled shoe that landed on the dashboard.

He said, "It's for the best," and eased away, the crowd parting to let him go, and was soon clear of them. He couldn't see her clearly in his rearview mirror, but thought she was on the street on her back, surrounded, kicking up at them.

Kept his head down as he drove through Clichy-sous-Bois, wipers smearing the spit into rainbow arcs across the glass, driving fast enough that most of the thrown bricks missed him. He thought he heard a gunshot as he turned a corner, but couldn't tell if the bullet had been aimed at him.

And somehow made it through to Livry-Gargan and the N3, which would take him to Paris. He parked well short of the exit, at a bus stop, wiped his prints off the steering wheel and gearshift, and left the car with the keys in it, doubting it would make it through the night.

Jimmy Two Bulls drank coffee with a trembling hand at a twenty-four-hour roadside restaurant and gas station near the exit to the N3. It took over an hour for his breath to come normally and not in shallow gasps. He tried to eat but couldn't. The black tumor inside him had stopped growing but was still there. He doubted it would ever leave.

He'd never know his son, but he now knew why the boy asked who his mother was. Jimmy couldn't answer the question in the dream, and couldn't answer it now. He had no fucking idea who she was.

They didn't bury aborted babies, did they? He doubted it. Probably burned them with the other medical waste in a clinical incinerator, the flames no different than the fire of a burning car.

There was a tap on his shoulder.

"*Parlez-vous français?*"

He turned. She was in her thirties, attractive, blond. It was obvious she'd been drinking, the way her eyes sparkled. Her girlfriend sat in a booth watching the exchange, a wolfish expression on her face. A pair of straw cowboy hats sat on the table between them—they'd been to the Wild West Show. Gotten all heated up, he guessed.

"*Ni glasses toki ye he?*" Jimmy said in Lakota. "*Ni* TV Guide *toki ya he?*"

She was obviously thrilled. He knew he could go home with them. Instead, he tossed one of the plane tickets in a trash can outside the door.

No, he explained with hand signals, he didn't want to go home with them. He wanted to go to the airport. He held out his arms so they looked like airplane wings. They agreed, reluctantly, to take him there, obviously disappointed.

Although they were talking over each other to him in French and he found himself recognizing a few of the words, his eyes were to the east, toward the dark maw of Clichy-sous-Bois, lit only by isolated fires, wondering how long it would take the flames to reach those who remained.

BLOOD KNOT

Fourteen-year-old Hattie Sykes was awake when her grandfather cracked the bedroom door ajar and said, "Ready to hit the river?"

Because he was deaf he spoke loudly, assuming everyone else was deaf as well. She could see he was wearing his fly-fishing clothes: old chest waders held up by suspenders, a thick red shirt, a fishing vest, a short-brimmed Stetson.

She said, "It's not even light out yet."

"Hell, I gave you an extra thirty minutes."

"What time is it?"

"Five forty-five. Damned late."

Hattie moaned. The room smelled of her brother Jake in the next bed. Nothing smelled as awful as a sixteen-year-old boy in a closed room.

"Anyone else coming?" he asked.

"No, they said they'd rather sleep in."

"I'm not surprised!" he boomed.

She watched as he missed with the egg. Instead of cracking it into the pan, the runny yolk and white slithered onto the burner. He cursed, caught himself, and said, "Sorry."

"Let me do it," she said, getting up from the table.

"My eyes don't work until they're warmed up," he said, stepping aside.

While she scrambled eggs on a clean burner and cleaned up the mess, he shuffled around the kitchen with a cup of coffee. She didn't like coffee but she liked the smell of it in the morning, especially in her grandfather's lodge. Especially before they went fishing.

Her two older brothers, Jake and Justin, were still sleeping downstairs. Justin was the oldest and landed the spare bedroom to himself. Her parents were in the master bedroom on the top floor. Her grandfather had given them that room because he no longer liked climbing the stairs. Plus, they liked to sleep late after a night spent emptying the liquor cabinet.

The sun broke over the mountains and lit up the dew on the grass like sequins. Her grandfather walked haltingly toward the river with his fly rod and she followed. He was a tall man with wide shoulders, but from the back he seemed to be caving in on himself. She'd seen photos of him when he was young, before he started his company, married her grandmother, raised her mother, and got rich. He was brash and dashing, with jet-black hair and high, almost Indian cheekbones. Those high cheekbones now made his face look skeletal, and his once-sharp eyes were filmy. A fleshy dewlap under his jaw swayed as he walked. Since her grandmother died the year before, he'd turned into an old man and he preferred to live at his lodge on the river rather than at his big house in town.

"I wrote a story at school," Hattie said. "I called it 'Fishing with My Grandpa.' "

"Did I catch a lot of big fish in it?" he asked.

"Well, one."

"I hope you got an A."

"I did."

In the car on the way to the lodge her parents had talked softly, assuming the three children were all sleeping. Hattie was faking it, and listened.

"I won't miss this annual pilgrimage to visit the old coot," her father said.

"I know," her mother agreed.

"This is probably the last year we can make the boys come," he said. "With no Wi-Fi or video games, what are they supposed to do? It's ridiculous."

"Jay . . ."

"Every year we pay homage," her dad said. "I hope to hell it's worth it for us in the end. Just another year or two, I think."

"It means a lot to him," her mother said.

"It better mean a lot to *us*."

"Hattie still likes it."

"She's going to grow up, too. And then what?"

She watched as her grandfather struggled to tie the tippet to the leader of his line. His fingers were long and bony, the backs of his hands mottled with spots. He couldn't see well enough to make a knot.

"Can I help?"

"Do you know how to tie a blood knot?"

"Yuck," she said, taking the two strands.

He laughed. "There's no blood involved."

He told her how to cross the lines over each other, twist the ends around the opposite length, and pull the tips through the loop to secure it. She was surprised at how well the knot turned out.

"It's not about blood," he said, thanking her, "it's about the knot."

He cast gracefully. He told her fly-fishing was an elegant sport, and she agreed. There was a V-shaped braided current in the river created by a rock. There was usually a fish there, but he wasn't presenting the fly far enough upstream.

She said, "More to your right."

He shifted his feet and squared his shoulders, cast again, and the fly drifted through the braid. She saw the trout come up out of the depths and take it.

"Fish on," he said, raising the tip of his rod to set the hook. She clapped her hands and was surprised when he handed the rod to her.

"Bring it in, Hattie," he said. "You can do it."

After landing the rainbow trout—it looked metallic and beautiful in the morning sun—she released it back into the water. She was thrilled, and when she stood up he slipped his fishing vest over her narrow shoulders.

"It's yours," he said. "The rod, too. Now catch another one."

As they walked back to the lodge at mid-morning, her parents were out on the deck drinking coffee in their robes. They looked disheveled. Her brothers weren't to be seen.

Her grandfather said, "The lodge needs to be stained every five years. The decks need to be painted every three. All the paperwork is in my desk."

She stopped and squinted at him.

"The keys are in the pocket of the vest," he said. "Maybe your mom and dad will come visit you once a year."

Hattie realized what was happening, but she couldn't speak. Her eyes stung with tears.

"It's not about blood," he said, brushing her cheek with the back of his hand. "It's about the knot."

SHOTS FIRED
A REQUIEM FOR
ANDER ESTI

On an unseasonably warm fall day in the eastern foothills of the Bighorn Mountains in Wyoming, game warden Joe Pickett heard the call from dispatch over his pickup radio:

"Please meet the reporting party on County Road 307 at the junction of County Road 62. RP claims he was attempting to cross public land when shots were fired in his direction. The RP claims his vehicle was struck by bullets. Assailant is unknown."

Joe paused a moment to let the message sink in, then snatched the mike from its cradle on the dashboard.

"This is GF-24. Are we talking about the junction up above Indian Paintbrush Basin?"

"Affirmative."

"I can be there in fifteen minutes," he said, glancing at his mirrors and pulling over to the side of the two-lane highway five miles west of Winchester. The highway was clear in both directions with the exception of a hay combine lumbering westbound a mile in front of him. His tires had been scattering loose stalks of hay since he'd turned off the interstate.

Joe drove into the borrow pit and swung the truck around in a U-turn. He knew of an old gravel two-track that would cut across swaths of public and ranch land and emerge on the crest of Indian Paintbrush Basin. The shortcut would save him twenty minutes as opposed to backtracking to the interstate and going around. If the sheriff were to respond, it would take at least forty-five minutes for a deputy to get out there from town.

Before the call had come, Joe was patrolling the northern flank of his district, keeping an eye out for a local miscreant named Bryce Pendergast, whom Joe had arrested the year before on assault and felony narcotics charges. Pendergast had been convicted and sent to the State Honor Farm in Riverton, but had recently walked away and was last seen climbing into a rusted-out white van driven by an unknown accomplice. A BOLO had been put out for him, and Joe surmised that Pendergast might visit his grandmother in Winchester, but it turned out he hadn't. The old woman said not only had Bryce not been there, but that he owed her $225, and if he showed up without it she would call the cops. Joe liked the idea of putting Bryce in jail twice.

But a live situation trumped a cold one.

"Are there any injuries?" Joe asked the dispatcher, knowing the conversation was likely being monitored by other game wardens across the State of Wyoming as well as law enforcement and nosy neighbors throughout Twelve Sleep County.

"Negative," the female dispatcher said. "The party reports bullet holes in the sidewall of his truck, but they didn't hit anybody."

"Yikes."

"I'll ask the RP to stay out of the line of fire but remain at the scene until you get there."

"Do you have a name for the RP?" Joe asked, flipping open his spiral notebook to a fresh page while driving down the rough road, then uncapping a pen with his teeth.

The name was Burton Hanks of Casper. While Joe bumped up and down in the cab, he scrawled the name and Hanks's cell phone number on the pad. His two-year-old yellow Labrador, Daisy, fixated on the wavery pen strokes as if she desperately wanted to snatch the pen out of his grip and chew it into oblivion, which she would if she got the chance.

"Did you run the name?" Joe asked the dispatcher.

"Affirmative. He's got a general license deer tag and said he is attempting to scout Area 25."

Joe nodded to himself. Area 25 was a massive and mountainous hunting area that included mountains, breaklands, and huge grassy swales. The official opening day was October 15, a few weeks away. Meaning Hanks was likely a trophy hunter out on a scout to identify the habitat of the biggest buck deer. Locals would literally wait

271

until the opener to go up there, but serious trophy hunters would be out well in advance to mark their territory.

Joe had mixed feelings when it came to serious trophy hunters, but he put them aside.

As he motored down the washboarded county road, leaving a plume of dust behind him, the issue wasn't scouting or trophy hunting or the ethics of trophy hunters. The issue was contained in two words: *shots fired*.

Before he reached the foothills to begin his climb into the timber and out the other side to Indian Paintbrush Basin, a herd of seventy to eighty pronghorn antelope looked up and watched him pass from where they grazed among the sagebrush. A herd that big—all does and fawns—meant there would be a bruiser of a buck somewhere watching over his harem, keeping them in line. Joe saw the buck over the next small hill. The animal was heavy-bodied and alert, with impressive curled horns with ivory tips and an alpha-male strut to his step.

Over the next hill, five young bachelor bucks, like pimply-faced adolescents with too much time on their hands and testosterone in their blood, milled about in a tight circle butting heads and, Joe assumed, plotting a coup attempt against the big buck to take charge of the harem. The bachelors strutted and butted at each other, and watched Joe go by with what looked like lopsided sneers.

Joe checked his wristwatch as he nosed his pickup through a steep-sided notch in the hill that would narrow ahead before the road climbed the last rise. It was two-thirty in the afternoon. He was expected home by six so he and his wife, Marybeth, could attend his daughter Lucy's musical at the Saddlestring High School. She was a costar in a politically correct production he'd never heard of and was scheduled to sing a song called "Diversity." He didn't want to miss it, yet he did. Nevertheless, he hoped the shots-fired incident could be resolved quickly enough that he could make it home on time.

As the road got rougher and he pitched about within the cab, Daisy placed both her paws on the dashboard for balance and stared through the front windshield as if to provide navigation support.

"Almost there," Joe said to her, shifting into four-wheel-drive low to climb the rise. The surface of the old two-track was dry and loose. He liked the idea of coming onto the scene from an unexpected direction. The sudden appearance of a green Game and Fish vehicle sometimes froze the parties in a dispute and gave him time to assess the situation on his own before confronting them or figuring out what to do. Most of all, it allowed him to see a situation with his own eyes before the involved parties weighed in.

• • •

He broke over the ridge and the vista to the east was clear and stunning: the foothills gave way to a huge bowl of grass miles across in every direction. The bowl—called Indian Paintbrush Swale, after the state's official flower—was rimmed on three sides by timbered mountains either dark with pine in shadow or bright green if fused with afternoon sun. Between the swale and where Joe cleared the ridge top was a late-model maroon Chevy Avalanche faux pickup parked just off the county road. Two men stood with their backs to him at first, then wheeled around, obviously surprised that he'd come from behind.

One of the men, standing near the front of the Avalanche, was tall and heavy with a long mustache that dropped to his jawline around both sides of his mouth. He wore a battered brown cowboy hat with a high crown and had a deeply creased and weathered face that indicated he either worked outside or spent a lot of his hours outdoors. The second man looked to be around the same age—fifty-five to sixty—but was clean-shaven and softer in features. He was hatless but wore a starched chamois shirt and new jeans that looked hours out of the box.

The man in the hat waved Joe over. The second man was obviously subordinate to the large man and hung back to stay out of the way and observe.

Joe put his pickup into park and let Daisy out.

The dog followed him a few inches from his boot heels and kept her head down, sniffing the grass and sagebrush along the way.

The man in the cowboy hat, Burton Hanks, said he was a little surprised Joe didn't know of him.

"I'm the guy who broke the Boone and Crockett record for a mule deer in Wyoming last fall," Hanks said. "Scored 201 and three-eighths overall. Six points on the right side and five on the left. The inside spread was twenty-eight and a quarter," he said proudly.

"No offense," Joe said, "but I don't pay much attention to records. I'm here because someone reported shots fired. I assume you're the reporting party."

Hanks was chastened, but said, "That's me."

"So," Joe said, "who was shooting at whom?"

"Some third-world asshole shot at us!" Hanks bellowed, gesturing toward his pickup. "All we were doing was starting to cross that basin down there. Come look at this if you don't believe me."

Joe followed Hanks around the Avalanche.

"Here's the evidence," Hanks said, pointing at the small bullet hole in the metal sheeting of the rear bumper guard.

"Yup," Joe said, leaning close to the bumper. The hole was clean and the bullet was likely lodged somewhere in the sidewall of the bed. "Eight inches lower and it would have hit the tire," Joe said.

"And five inches higher and it might have punctured the fuel line and blown us to kingdom come," Hanks added. "Here, there's another one," he said, pressing his index finger against a second hole in the sidewall a few feet in back of the cab. The bullet had pierced the outside sheet metal and exited on the top rail of the pickup bed, leaving angry sharp tongues of steel. Which meant the shot had been fired from a lower elevation than the truck at the time, Joe thought.

"Let me get a couple of pictures," Joe said, returning to his own truck for his digital camera. "Did you get a look at who did the shooting?"

"Hell yes," Hanks said. "And you can put away that camera, Warden. I can point you at who shot at us and you can go down there and arrest him right now."

Joe said, "You mean he's still there?"

"That's what I'm saying. You can borrow my binocs and I'll point him out to you."

Joe was surprised. Previously, a series of likely scenarios had circled around in the back of his mind: the shooter was also a trophy hunter intending to spook the competition; the shooter was zeroing in his rifle when the Avalanche got in the way; the shooter was poaching elk and was surprised by the intrusion. It didn't occur to him that the shooter would still be in the basin twenty minutes later.

He frowned. The last thing he needed—or

wanted—was a situation where a man with a rifle was hidden away in isolated terrain. A whole new set of scenarios—more dangerous than the first set—began to emerge. Joe knew that by the time the sheriff's department arrived, the shooter could either escape or bunker in for a long standoff.

Hanks handed Joe a pair of Zeiss Victory 8×42 binoculars and arched his eyebrows in anticipation of a compliment. The binoculars were known to be the best, and were among the most expensive optics available, at over $2,000 a pair. Joe took them and refrained from commenting on them. But looking through them was like being transported into a clearer and sharper world than what was available to the naked eye.

Joe swept the grassy basin and the lenses filled with the backs of hundreds of sheep he hadn't noticed before. The herd was so large it had melded into the scenery of the basin but now it was obvious. The sheep were moving only a few inches at a time as they grazed on the grass, heads down, like a huge cumulus cloud barely moving across the sky. Unlike cattle, sheep snipped the grass close to the surface and left the range with the appearance of a manicured golf green. Which is one of the primary reasons sheepmen and cattlemen had gone to war over a century before.

"All I see is sheep," Joe said to Hanks.

"Keep going," Hanks said. "Look right square in the middle of that basin."

Joe found a distant structure of some kind and focused in.

"The sheep wagon?" Joe said.

The ancient wagon was parked in the middle of the giant swale. It had a rounded sheet metal top painted white that fit like a muffin top on a squared-off frame. Sheep wagons were hitched to vehicles and towed to where the herds were and left, sometimes for weeks. They had long tongues for towing, water barrels cinched to the sides, small windows on the sides of the metal cover skin, and narrow double doors on the front. The black snout of a chimney pipe poked through the roof.

There wasn't a pickup parked beside the wagon but a saddled horse was tied to a picket pin, as well as a black-and-white blue heeler dog.

"That's where the shots came from," Hanks said.

"And all you were doing was going down the road minding your own business?"

"I don't like the insinuation," Hanks said haughtily. "We were driving on a county road through private land, legal as hell. When I drove the Avalanche down there from up here, I heard the first bullet hit before I even heard a shot. Then the second one hit. I stopped the truck and glassed the basin and saw that sheep wagon. The guy who shot at us had the top door open on the wagon and I could see a rifle barrel sticking out. I never saw him clearly. He didn't close the door until we hightailed it back up here and called 911."

Joe lowered the binoculars and handed them back. "You're sure you didn't do anything to provoke him?" he asked. "Were you spooking his sheep?"

"I goddamned told you exactly what happened," Hanks said, turning to his friend. "Isn't that right, Bill? I didn't leave anything out, did I?"

Bill said, "Nope. All we were doing was driving along the road and that nut down there started popping off at us. We didn't threaten him or nothing. And we weren't even close to his sheep yet."

"Why are you even asking these questions?" Hanks said to Joe. "Don't you believe us? You saw the bullet holes."

"I did. But this is the first time I ever heard of him getting aggressive and shooting at somebody."

"You know him?" Hanks asked, incredulous.

"His name is Ander Esti. I recognize his horse. He's been around this country for a long time—before I ever got here. He's not the type to just shoot at somebody."

"Well, this time he did, Warden," Hanks said.

Joe nodded. He could detect no discrepancies in their story, although he couldn't yet be sure.

"Where are you boys staying in town?" Joe asked.

Hanks said the Holiday Inn.

"Why don't you go on back there for now. I'll drive down and talk to Ander and I'll bring him in to the county jail. I'll stop by the Holiday Inn on my way home and let you know where things stand."

Hanks and Bill looked at each other, obviously a little suspicious of the methodology Joe had suggested.

"Go back, relax, have a beer," Joe said. "There's no reason for the three of us to go charging down there. Ander Esti is . . . well . . . a unique individual. He can get a little excitable—"

"That's fucking obvious," Hanks huffed.

"There's no need to spook him," Joe continued. "I think I can handle this best on my own and I'll let you know how it goes."

Hanks turned somber. "Are you sure you don't want me to cover you? I have my .308 Winchester Mag along with me," he said, chinning toward the Avalanche. "Bill brought along his AR-15."

Joe hardened his expression and said, "If you stick around here much longer, I'll need to start asking you two why you brought your hunting rifle along a month before the season opens."

Hanks and Bill looked at each other, and that seemed to settle it. Joe guessed Hanks to be one of those trophy hunters who maybe just couldn't pass up a record-setting buck even if it was before the season opened. They agreed to meet Joe later and climbed into their Avalanche and started the slow, four-wheel-drive trek back to the highway.

When the Avalanche was out of view, Joe said to Daisy, "There's something wrong here."

The first time Joe met Ander Esti was on a similarly warm September day eight years before. Joe was assisting an exploration survey crew hired by the state to confirm corner posts and benchmarks that had been established in the 1890s, when the state was first mapped by the U.S. Geological Survey. The crew needed to reestablish property lines in the Pumpkin Buttes area for a new plat of the ownership of private and state lands. Because Joe was the warden for the district and knew the territory as well as most of the local landowners, he was asked to be on call if there were access issues for the survey crew, who had flown in from Virginia and were completely new to the vast and empty terrain.

When one of the surveyors did his triangulation of a possible benchmark from a hilltop, he determined that the ground they needed to stake happened to fall right in the middle of a sheep wagon that had been parked in a semi-arid mountain valley. The surveyor was uncomfortable approaching the wagon—he'd never seen such a thing in his life—and told Joe he'd witnessed a man wading through a herd of sheep with a rifle resting on his shoulder. So Joe volunteered to approach the sheepherder and suggest that together they could roll the wagon a few feet forward or back so a survey stake could be driven into the ground.

Joe knew at the time that the best way to approach sheepherders—who were often left with the herds for weeks at a time—was head-on and as obvious as possible. The men employed by ranchers to tend the massive herds were often Basque and some barely spoke English. Fresh water and food was delivered to them every ten days to two weeks by the rancher who employed the Basques. Because of their lack of human interaction, they could become isolated and jumpy, especially when coyotes or eagles were preying on the stock. Rarely was a sheepherder in a situation where his rifle wasn't within reach.

So Joe drove slowly and deliberately toward the wagon, letting the stock part out of the way in front of his truck. As he neared the wagon he got out and shut his pickup door with a bang and called out. Although there was a saddled horse tied to the side of the wagon and a curl of smoke from the chimney pipe, the door didn't open and the curtains inside didn't rustle, even though it was the middle of the day.

He walked up to the wagon with his right hand on the grip of his weapon, but removed it when he reached the door. If the sheepherder looked out and saw him standing there with his hand on his gun, he didn't want to appear to provoke him. As he reached up to knock on the door, he heard a pair of voices coming from inside. Joe paused.

They were speaking in Spanish, Basque Spanish. It was obvious from the back-and-forth cadence that one man was telling the other a series of jokes. The second man found the jokes hilariously funny, and snorted when he laughed. He laughed so hard the wagon rocked.

Two herders in one wagon was unusual, Joe thought, but not unprecedented. The inside of a sheep wagon was spartan and simple—a table with a bench seat on each side, a compact pantry and cupboard at floor level, a small woodstove for cooking, and a raised bunk at the back for sleeping—perhaps the earliest version of a camper trailer. Two normal-sized men inside would likely find the situation suffocating.

Joe knocked on the door and instantly the joking stopped.

He waited a beat, and knocked again and identified himself.

Finally, there was a scuff of boots on the plank-wood floor inside and the top door swung open to reveal a dark and compact man in a snap-button cowboy shirt, a loose silk bandanna hanging from his neck, and black eyes so small and intense that Joe stepped back.

It was Ander Esti, and he was alone and it was

obvious he was just finishing up his lunch. He'd been telling jokes to himself. And laughing.

After they'd rolled the wagon ten feet back, Joe asked Ander if he often told jokes to himself. Esti gestured that he didn't understand the question, and Joe let it drop.

Later, during the winter, Joe spotted Ander in the front row of their church during services. The man sat alone wearing a clean but ancient snap-button western shirt and he appeared to listen intently to the minister. He left after services, before Joe could talk to him, and he showed up again seven weeks later.

Joe asked the minister about the man, and the reverend chuckled and said Ander attended a different church every week in Saddlestring and was on his second rotation of the winter. He was generous with his donation in the plate but had no interest in joining. And he wouldn't show up again once the snows melted and the ranchers were hiring.

Ander Esti was the kind of character, Joe came to find out, who moved through the community and somehow left no impression he'd ever been there. During the winter months, he'd be on the periphery of the small Christmas parade put on by the downtown merchants or alone in the top row of the high school basketball game. He never spoke to anyone, and when he was gone no one recalled he'd been there.

Ander seemed to float through the seasons with a light footprint and a particular pattern: work all summer and fall in the high country without a day off, then winter in town like a ghost, slowly spending the wages he'd made until it was summer again. He was self-sufficient and never applied for unemployment insurance or welfare when he didn't work, and never showed up for free lunch at the community center.

Joe noticed him, though, because he made a point of it. But he never got to know the man well and never had a conversation with him. And when he waved at Ander, the man appeared not to recognize him.

The sheep wagon Joe approached was the same unit where he'd originally met Ander but even more in need of a new coat of paint. Shards of green were curling off the base of the wagon and windows of galvanized metal could be seen on the sloped roof. It was warm enough that there was no curl of smoke from the stove. Ander Esti's roan gelding looked thinner than the last time, and his dog more vicious.

Joe grabbed the mike from the dashboard and called it in. Because he was in the swale, reception was poor and filled with static.

"This is GF-24," he said to the dispatcher two

hundred and fifty miles away in Cheyenne. "I'm approaching the scene of the incident. It's a sheep wagon belonging to the C Lazy U Ranch north of Kaycee. The perp in question appears to be inside and I know him. His name is Ander Esti . . ." Joe spelled out the name.

"Are you requesting backup?" the dispatcher asked.

Joe smiled to himself. "Negative. I'll call in when I'm clear."

Like before, Joe made sure his presence was known as he neared the wagon. He braked twenty yards from the front. Despite what the two hunters had claimed, Joe couldn't imagine Esti being hostile. Nevertheless, he checked the loads in his shotgun before climbing out, but decided not to carry it to the front door of the wagon. Instead, he propped it inside the open door of his pickup. As he walked toward the front of the wagon, he touched the grip of his Glock with his fingertips but left it in the holster. He couldn't conceive of a need to draw it out.

The sheep on all sides created a cacophony of mewls and abrasive calls. The blue heeler growled at him, showing its teeth and straining and lunging at a leash rope. The dog seemed unnaturally aggressive and upset, Joe thought.

Hundreds of sheep surrounded the wagon. They were so tightly packed together that they looked and functioned as a two-and-a-half-foot containment wall. Joe could hear them munching dry grass, and the sound became a low hum in the background.

"Ander? It's Joe Pickett," he called out as he neared the wagon but stopped well short of the dog. "Ander, you need to come out so we can talk. Some guys scouting for elk said you shot at their truck. They're gone now—it's just me."

Although there were no sounds from inside, Joe noticed a very subtle shift in the wagon—weight being transferred from side to side, as if Esti was pacing. But it couldn't be pacing because there wasn't enough floor space. He must be shifting from the stool near the door to the bench at the table, Joe thought. He tried to picture Ander inside. The man was probably guilt-ridden and anxious about what he'd done. Joe couldn't imagine what might go through a man's mind after months of isolation with only a horse, a dog, and hundreds of sheep to talk to. Or what a man might think if he looked up and saw a strange pickup in the distance.

"Ander, come on out, but leave your rifle inside. Open your door so we can talk."

Joe heard an impatient sigh and the latch of the upper door being thrown.

And Bryce Pendergast stood there holding Ander Esti's lever-action carbine, pointing it directly at Joe's face. Pendergast's head was shaved and there were new tattoos on his neck

287

and temple. He was shaking with rage or fear or meth and his eyes were wide open and wild.

Behind him, in the wagon, a female voice said, "Just shoot the motherfucker, Bryce. Just shoot him now."

"Shut the fuck up!" Pendergast hissed to the woman. Then to Joe: "So, it's *you*."

Joe felt the blood in his face drain out and the hairs on the back of his neck rise.

"Where's Ander?" Joe asked. "Do you have him with you in there?"

"Who?" Pendergast asked, his voice high and tight.

"Ander Esti. The sheepherder."

"So that's his name," Pendergast said.

Joe wondered what exactly that meant.

"Okay, Game Warden," Pendergast said, as he dropped his left hand from the front stock of the rifle but kept it aimed at Joe. "You need to unbuckle that belt and let it drop to the ground. Do it slow."

Joe swallowed hard. He'd screwed up by forgetting his training and letting his familiarity with Ander Esti soften his approach. *Never assume,* he'd been taught. But he'd assumed.

He reached down and undid his belt and let his Glock, cuffs, bear spray, and extra magazines thump to the ground.

"I remember that goddamned bear spray,"

Pendergast said, undoing the latch to the lower door and kicking it open. "It nearly fuckin' blinded me."

"I remember," Joe said.

Joe recalled the takedown, when he was surprised by an armed Pendergast on the threshold of a rental house, and the first thing he was able to grab to protect himself was the canister of bear spray. And he remembered Pendergast writhing on the lawn, sobbing and crying that his rights had been violated.

Pendergast asked, "How'd you like that shit in *your* eyes?"

"I wouldn't."

Pendergast snorted and stepped down out of the wagon. The muzzle of the rifle trembled because Pendergast trembled. Joe looked at the man closely: wild eyes, flushed cheeks, sinew-like taut cords in his neck, veins popping on his forearms.

As Pendergast cleared the door, Joe caught a glimpse of a skinny and dirty blonde inside, peeking out. She had long stringy hair and eyes as wild as Bryce's. A tweaker, Joe thought. A couple of tweakers.

"Where's Ander?" Joe asked.

Pendergast ignored him. He backed Joe up and squatted—with the rifle still aimed at Joe's chest—to retrieve the gear belt and holstered pistol. He tossed it behind him so it landed in a coil beneath the wagon.

"We're gonna be taking your pickup out of here," Pendergast said. "Is there plenty of gas in it?"

"Yup," Joe said. "But it won't be as easy as that."

Pendergast shook his head. "Why the hell not?"

"It's a law enforcement vehicle," Joe explained, dancing as fast as he could. "It's got a GPS black box inside. The suits at headquarters can track it if it moves even a foot from where it is right now. So if it moves, they have to call me for a check-in. If you take my truck and don't answer when they call in, they'll know you've stolen it and they'll send out a tracker plane or helicopter. You can't just take a law enforcement vehicle anymore."

Pendergast seemed flummoxed, but he covered himself by saying, "Yeah, I guess I heard something about that."

"So if you want to go somewhere, I'll be happy to drive you," Joe said. "But you can't just leave me here and take it if you don't want to get caught."

"Maybe you're going with us," Pendergast said, narrowing his eyes.

"I thought that's what I just said." Joe grinned. Then: "So was it you who shot a couple of rounds at a pickup a while back?" Joe asked, keeping his tone conversational. "The guy who called it in said he thought it was the sheepherder."

"It was Bryce," the woman said from inside the wagon. "Ain't that right, honey?" She was proud of him.

Pendergast nodded in agreement but kept his eyes locked on Joe.

"Get out here," Pendergast said to the woman. "I need your help."

"Doing what?" she asked.

"Just get the fuck out here," Pendergast shouted.

"Jesus, you don't need to yell," she said, stepping out. Joe recognized her. He'd seen her playing girls' basketball a couple of years ahead of his oldest daughter, Sheridan, for the same Saddlestring Wranglerette team. But she looked twenty-five years older than she should. He could see yellowed stubs where her row of white teeth used to be when she opened her mouth. She seemed to notice him staring and clamped her mouth shut. She was a serious meth user, all right. And maybe, he thought, she recognized *him*.

"So what did you do with Ander?" Joe asked. "I see his horse here and his dog."

"Shut the hell up," Pendergast said.

"So since your white van isn't anywhere around here," Joe said, "I'm guessing you broke down or got stuck somewhere close and walked until you found the sheep wagon. You were probably hoping there'd be a vehicle with it, but there wasn't. So what did you do with Ander?"

"I said shut up while I think."

"Never your strong suit," Joe said. "But I'm worried about Ander. He's known as a hard worker and a good guy, even if he's a little . . . off. I've never met a rancher around here who didn't want to hire him. He takes his job seriously and he never caused anyone any problems. He keeps to himself and works hard for a day's pay. He's trustworthy and honest and he's never hurt or screwed anyone. I'd hate to think that something happened to him, because anyone who knew him liked the man.

"So," Joe asked, "do you know where he is?"

Pendergast paused for a moment, then screamed, *"Quit fucking asking the questions. I got the rifle—so I ask the questions."*

"Okay," Joe said.

The girl shuffled up behind and to the left of Pendergast. Joe noticed for the first time that she held an old Colt .45 revolver in her hands. He glanced over his shoulder toward the open door of the wagon. No Ander. But he could see meth-smoking paraphernalia on the small table inside—crumpled aluminum foil packets, stubby pipes, open books of matches.

"Who knows you're here?" Pendergast said.

Joe weighed his answer before he said, "Plenty of folks. I gave my location to the dispatcher just a few minutes ago. The sheriff's department and the highway patrol are on their way. I'd suggest we end this before something bad happens."

"When will they get here?" Pendergast asked, alarmed.

"Any minute," Joe said.

Pendergast broke his glare and scanned the terrain for vehicles. "I don't hear nobody coming."

Joe shrugged. "Lots of folks are looking for you since you walked away from the Honor Farm. The best way to go here would be to put down the rifle and turn yourself in. That way you'll be cooperating and they might go easy on you."

"Fuck that," Pendergast said, spitting out the words. "I ain't going back there. You know what they had me doin' on that farm? Milking fucking cows. I hate cows. I ain't no farmer."

Joe nodded. Bryce Pendergast had been raised well by solid parents. He had two brothers and a sister who had turned out all right. Bryce was in the middle, and had always been a wreck. Couldn't keep a job, car theft, parole violations. He'd been in the process of setting up a meth lab with a buddy when Joe first arrested him.

"No, you aren't a farmer," Joe said.

Pendergast pursed his mouth and nodded as if they'd finally agreed on something. Then he seemed to recall why he'd asked the girl to come out of the wagon.

"Kelsey, put your gun on him for a minute."

Kelsey—Joe now remembered her name as Kelsey Trocker—looked confused.

"What do you mean, *on* him?" she asked.

Pendergast sighed and said, "Raise that pistol and cock the hammer back and aim it at his face. If he so much as flinches, you pull the trigger. Now do you fuckin' understand?"

"Yeah," she said, "but you don't need to talk to me like that."

"Just do it."

"Where you goin'?"

"I gotta pee."

"Oh, okay."

Pendergast stepped aside while Kelsey stepped forward. Joe felt his life about to end when she raised the revolver and fumbled with the hammer in an effort to cock it. She was as shaky as Pendergast. Then she managed to figure it out and Joe watched the cylinder rotate and the hammer lock in place. He could see—close as he was—lead bullets in three of the four visible chambers. The chamber that previously had been lined up in the barrel had been fired.

And he thought he knew what had happened to Ander Esti.

Pendergast kept his eyes on Joe while he backed away, making sure Kelsey had the situation under control. Then he turned near the wagon and Joe could hear him unzipping his jeans.

"Did you shoot Ander?" Joe asked in a low voice.

She shook her head no, but something that scared her flashed through her eyes. Maybe she was just now remembering what they'd done . . .

"You don't need to go down with him," Joe said, chinning toward Pendergast. "If Bryce was the one who did it, you can get yourself out of this."

"Shut up," she said, and Joe could see her finger whiten on the trigger. He shut up.

After leaving a meager puddle in the dirt, Pendergast zipped up and hoisted the rifle. He strode back toward Joe, but then stopped, as if he suddenly recalled something. With a lopsided grin, he turned and found Joe's gear belt and removed the canister of bear spray.

Joe thought, *Oh no.*

"Keep that gun on him," Pendergast said to Kelsey, as he clamped the rifle under his left arm. He held the bear spray aloft in his right hand.

"How'd you like a taste of your own goddamn medicine?" he said to Joe.

"I wouldn't."

"You thought it was pretty damned funny when you used it on me."

"No, I didn't," Joe said.

"I learned at the Farm that this stuff," he said, gesturing to the canister, "ain't even legal to use on a human. It's too damned powerful. They shoulda arrested you for excess force for sprayin' me."

"It was self-defense," Joe said. "You might remember you were trying to shoot me at the time."

"Bryce," Kelsey said, stepping back, "don't get any of that stuff on *me*."

"Don't worry, darlin'," Pendergast said, warming up to his idea. "Just don't take that gun off him."

"Be careful," Joe said to Pendergast. "That spray doesn't always go where you aim it."

Which made Pendergast pause for a moment while he studied the canister in his hand. There was a ring to put his index finger through, and a safety tab to flip up so he could trigger the release with his thumb. The complexity of it seemed to overwhelm him, Joe thought.

"Why don't you—" Kelsey started to say.

"Why don't you shut the fuck up!" Pendergast exploded. "He fucked me up with this stuff, so I'm gonna return the favor. Got it?"

Kelsey grimaced, and for a second the muzzle of the gun wavered.

"Really," Joe said helpfully, "sometimes it shoots out about forty-five degrees from where you aim it. So you've really got to know what you're doing."

It was about the fifth lie he'd told them since he arrived, he thought.

"Honey, can't you spray him later?" Kelsey pleaded.

Pendergast ignored her and advanced with the canister out in front of him. When it was three feet from Joe's face, Pendergast squeezed the trigger.

But because he hadn't armed the spray by raising the tab, nothing happened.

But Kelsey didn't know that. She'd covered her face with her left hand and closed her eyes to avoid blowback. Joe threw himself at her.

He wrenched the Colt free and bodychecked her with his hip and she fell away like a rag doll. Before Pendergast could get rid of the canister and reseat his rifle, Joe raised the .45 in Pendergast's general direction and fired.

The gunshot was flat and loud and Pendergast went down as if the wires that had held him aloft had been snipped. Joe didn't know where he'd hit him, but he thumbed back the hammer again and pounced. Pendergast had taken his rifle down with him and Joe didn't want it aimed at him.

Pendergast grunted *"Fuck-fuck-fuck-fuck"* and rolled in the dirt away from Joe, who could see a red stain blossoming through the fabric of Pendergast's pant leg near his knee. He looked as if he intended to roll to his backside and sit up so he could fire the rifle at Joe.

Joe shot him in the butt from three feet away and Pendergast howled.

The rifle barrel raised in the air and Joe grasped it with his left hand and jerked it away, then sent it flying toward the near flock of sheep that had frozen and watched them with dumb eyes.

When the rifle hit the backs of the sheep—they were that tightly packed together—the entire herd panicked and began to move away as if they were a single organism. Their bawls filled the air and thousands of tiny chunks of earth were kicked up by their sharp hooves and rained down near the wagon and on Joe and Pendergast and Kelsey.

"Ungh," Pendergast moaned, "you shot me in the ass."

"Yup," Joe said, cocking the hammer of the single-action.

Kelsey had recovered from being thrown aside and was on her hands and knees, trying to stand up.

"Just stay down," Joe said to her.

She sighed and did as she was told, but raised her head and stared at the grass where the sheep had been. "It wasn't me who shot that old man," she said vacantly. "All I was in this thing for was to pick up Bryce when he got loose so we could go to California, where I've got friends. But no—Bryce wanted to see his old grandma first and said he knew a back way. He got my van stuck in the mud because he was too fucked up to drive. Then we had to walk all the way here and . . ."

Joe followed her gaze and there he was. Ander Esti's body lay on its back not fifty feet from the wagon. His sheep had grazed around him and obscured him from view. There was no doubt from the odd angles of his arms that he was dead. That, and the hole in his forehead singed with a gunshot powder burn. The rifle Joe had flung—

Esti's ancient lever-action carbine—was in the dirt next to him.

Joe took a deep breath. He kept an eye on both tweakers while he released Esti's blue heeler, who bolted for where the body was and sat down beside it as if guarding the remains.

Pendergast had rolled onto his side so his wounded butt cheek was off the ground. He moaned and gasped and said again, "You shot me in the ass."

Joe said, "And I might just shoot you again."

With Kelsey cuffed to the front bumper and Pendergast cuffed to a ringbolt in the bed of his pickup, Joe called in the incident and requested a Life Flight helicopter as well as the sheriff's department crime scene team.

"The sheriff's department advises it may take an hour to get there," the dispatcher said. "They're worried about the suspect bleeding out."

Joe acknowledged the transmission and looked over the wall of his pickup bed at Pendergast, who had heard it.

"No great loss," Joe said, and keyed off.

"That was fucking cold," Pendergast said. But the bleeding had slowed since Joe had lifted him into the bed and wrapped the wounds. Most of the blood had flowed from Pendergast's broken knee, and Joe was able to cinch it securely. The buttocks entry shot seeped black blood like a puncture wound, and it didn't appear life-threatening.

Joe said to Pendergast, "You won't be able to just walk away next time you feel like it, either. This time, you'll go to big-boy prison in Rawlins and you'll be there for a long time."

Pendergast grimaced and looked away. He said, "There's a pipe in that wagon. I need a hit to kill the pain, so do me a solid, won't you?"

Joe turned away with thoughts of grabbing his shotgun and finishing the job.

Joe coaxed the story out of Kelsey.

After they'd gotten the van stuck and tried in vain half the day to dig it out with twisted lengths of greasewood, they'd set out on foot cross-country in the general direction of Winchester. After several hours, they saw the big herd of sheep and the wagon. Bryce figured there would be a pickup truck there as well, probably on the side of the wagon they couldn't see, and they'd threaten the sheepherder and get his keys.

Ander opened the door and said something they couldn't understand. Kelsey said it sounded like a foreign language but she couldn't be sure because she was so fucked up. Bryce ordered the man to speak English. When he didn't, Bryce took Kelsey's gun, which she'd stolen from her grandfather before driving south to pick up Bryce, and shot Ander in the forehead. They dragged his body into the herd of sheep thinking, she said, the sheep would eat it and destroy the evidence.

"You didn't know sheep don't eat meat?" Joe asked.

"How were we supposed to know *that?*" she said, rolling her eyes.

"I told you," Pendergast interjected, *"I ain't no farmer."*

Ander Esti's blue heeler wouldn't let Joe get close enough to put a sheet over the body. He looked back at his pickup and Daisy, who watched him through the passenger window.

He wondered if Daisy would stand guard over his own body if it came to it. He thought maybe she would.

When Joe came back to the pickup, the adrenaline rush that had enveloped him was fading into anger and melancholy. Pendergast looked up, his face a mask of pain and shock. Before he could speak, before he could beg Joe for a hit from his pipe, Joe said:

"That man you killed for nothing was one of the last of his kind. Those kind of men don't hardly exist anymore. As far as I know, he doesn't have a single family member to mourn him—just a few ranchers who won't be able to hire anyone to do what he did because no one will do it anymore. I didn't really know him and I don't know if anyone else did, either, except for his dog and his horse, and they aren't saying."

Pendergast whispered, "I don't know what the fuck you're talking about."

"Of course you don't," Joe said. "You're too thick and stupid. Men like Ander keep this world running. You never worked an honest day in your life and all you've ever cared about is your next high. You just take things, and you took that man's life. You murdered a man who did nothing but work. He never hurt a single soul. There is probably a lot more to him that I'll never know. But I won't get the chance to find out."

Pendergast looked away. He said, "I don't have to listen to this shit."

"No," Joe said, "but if I somehow could trade his life for yours, I'd do it."

As if choreographed, the still evening was broken by the chopping sound of the approaching helicopter and the grind of a sheriff's department SUV on the ridge above Indian Paintbrush Basin.

The sheep ignored the disruption. They'd long before bowed their heads to eat.

Center Point Large Print
600 Brooks Road / PO Box 1
Thorndike, ME 04986-0001 USA

(207) 568-3717

US & Canada:
1 800 929-9108
www.centerpointlargeprint.com